What Reviewers Say About Bold Strokes Books

"With its expected unexpected twists, vivid characters and healthy dose of humor, *Blind Curves* is a very fun read that will keep you guessing." – *Bay Windows*

"In a succinct film style narrative, with scenes that move, a character-driven plot, and crisp dialogue worthy of a screenplay ... the Richfield and Rivers novels are ... an engaging Hollywood mystery ... series." – *Midwest Book Review*

Force of Nature "...is filled with nonstop, fast paced action. Tornadoes, raging fire blazes, heroic and daring rescues... Baldwin does a fine job of describing the fast-paced scenes and inspiring the reader to keep on turning the pages." – *L-word.comLiterature*

In the Jude Devine mystery series the "...characters seem fully capable of walking away from the particulars of whodunit and engaging the reader in other aspects of their lives." – *Lambda Book Report*

Mine "...weaves a tale of yearning, love, lust, and conflict resolution ... a believable plot, with strong characters in a charming setting." – *JustAboutWrite*

"While these two women struggle with their issues, there is some very, very hot sex. If you enjoy complex characters and passionate sex scenes, you'll love *Wild Abandon*." – *MegaScene*

"*Course of Action* is a romance ... populated with a host of captivating and amiable characters. The glimpses into the lifestyles of the rich and beautiful people are rather like guilty pleasures ... a most satisfying and entertaining reading experience." – *Midwest Book Review*

The Clinic is "...a spellbinding novel." – *JustAboutWrite*

"*Unexpected Sparks* lived up to its promise and was thoroughly enjoyable ... Dartt did a lovely job at building the relationship between Kate and Nikki." – *Lambda Book Report*

"*Sequestered Hearts* ... is everything a romance should be. It is teeming with longing, heartbreak, and of course, love. As pure romances go, it is one of the best in print today." – *L-word.comLiterature*

"*The Exile and the Sorcerer* is a mesmerizing read, a tour-de-force packed with adventure, ordeals, complex twists and turns, and the internal introspection of appealing characters." – *Midwest Book Review*

The Spanish Pearl is "...both science fiction and romance in this adventurous tale ... A most entertaining read, with a sequel already in the works. Hot, hot, hot!" – *Minnesota Literature*

"A deliciously sexy thriller ... *Dark Valentine* is funny, scary, and very realistic. The story is tightly written and keeps the reader gripped to the exciting end." – *JustAbout Write3*

"*Punk Like Me* ... is different. It is engaging. It is life-affirming. Frankly, it is genius. This is a rare book in that it has a soul; one that is laid bare for all to see." – *JustAboutWrite*

"*Chance* is not a novel about the music industry; it is about a woman discovering herself as she muddles through all the trappings of fame." – *Midwest Book Review*

Sweet Creek "... is sublimely in tune with the times." – *Q-Syndicate*

"*Forever Found* ... neatly combines hot sex scenes, humor, engaging characters, and an exciting story." – *MegaScene*

Shield of Justice is a "...well-plotted...lovely romance...I couldn't turn the pages fast enough!" – Ann Bannon, author of *The Beebo Brinker Chronicles*

The 100th Generation is "...filled with ancient myths, Egyptian gods and goddesses, legends, and, most wonderfully, it contains the lesbian equivalent of Indiana Jones living and working in modern Egypt." – *Just About Write*

Sword of the Guardian is "...a terrific adventure, coming of age story, a romance, and tale of courtly intrigue, attempted assassination, and gender confusion ... a rollicking fun book and a must-read for those who enjoy courtly light fantasy in a medieval-seeming time." – *Midwest Book Review*

"*Of Drag Kings and the Wheel of Fate*'s lush rush of a romance incorporates reincarnation, a grounded transman and his peppy daughter, and the dark moods of a troubled witch—wonderful homage to Leslie Feinberg's classic gender-bending novel, *Stone Butch Blues*." – *Q-Syndicate*

In *Running with the Wind* "...the discussions of the nature of sex, love, power, and sexuality are insightful and represent a welcome voice from the view of late-20-something characters today." – *Midwest Book Review*

"Rich in character portrayal, *The Devil Inside* is an unusual, unpredictable, and thought-provoking love story that will have the reader questioning the definition of right and wrong long after she finishes the book." – *JustAboutWrite*

Wall of Silence "...is perfectly plotted and has a very real voice and consistently accurate tone, which is not always the case with lesbian mysteries." – *Midwest Book Review*

FALLING STAR

by

Gill McKnight

2008

This Trade Paperback Original Is Published By
Bold Strokes Books, Inc.
New York, USA

First Edition: July 2008

Credits
Editors: Jennifer Knight and Stacia Seaman
Production Design: Stacia Seaman
Cover Design By Sheri (graphicartist2020@hotmail.com)

Acknowledgments

In the BSB family I'd like to particularly thank Jennifer Knight, Rad, and Cate Culpepper for helping me find my feet and offering a steadying hand. I was very lucky to find you.

I'd also like to thank Ruth, Georgi, Lisa, Rae, and Pam for beta reading so long ago. I was very lucky to find you, too.

And a special thanks to Sheri for making the cover design fun.

Visit us at www.boldstrokesbooks.com

Dedication

For Effy, who said "Go on, try it."

CHAPTER ONE

T hree helicopters burst into view around the crest of Topaz Bay. Two large, militaristic-looking machines flanked a smaller civilian craft. The choppers swayed and spun out across the water, the noise from their engines reverberating in a low hum off the high coastal rise. Their waspish dance went on for several minutes as they jockeyed for position, until the center craft abruptly swooped lower and a dark, compact figure dropped out of it and plummeted into the ocean below.

Solley Rayner's chicken wing froze halfway to her mouth as she joined in the collective gasp of the family members around her. What just happened? Had they all just witnessed a horrific accident in the middle of their picnic? And on the very first day of their vacation? Concerned that her three children had inadvertently experienced an awful, psychologically damaging event, she was stunned when her sister Janie began to whoop and clap. The kids were jumping up and down, apparently thrilled that someone had fallen out of a helicopter and, splat, into the ocean. Even Nelson, the Irish red setter, barked himself senseless.

Janie's partner, Marsha, said their new pup had a brain the size of a pea, which didn't speak highly of Solley's IQ since the animal obviously knew something she didn't.

"You go, girl," Janie cried as the small figure swilling around in the water reached for the extended hoist lowered from the chopper above and was hauled slowly upward.

"You're kidding me. That's a movie stunt?" Solley finally caught on. She felt incredibly stupid; after all, they had come down to the beach to watch the filming. It was just that she hadn't expected, well...*that*.

"That's a water bomb," her son Jed said with relish. "You hit the water at about forty-five miles per vertical yard. If you don't hit it just right, you can break your back like a matchstick."

Solley thought about upping the parental locks on the home computer. Too much of the wrong sort of information seemed to be seeping into her older boy's head.

"Is she going to do it again?" her younger son Will asked.

"Again and again and again until Gin's happy it's perfect," Marsha said. "This could take all afternoon. I've even seen this type of thing carry over to the next day."

"Gin?" Solley queried.

"Yeah. Gin Ito, the stuntwoman," Marsha replied. "She's my best bud."

"Gin Ito?" Jed was wide-eyed. "Aunt Marsha, do you really know her?"

Bemused by her son's ardent response to this woman's name, Solley asked, "Who's Gin Ito?"

Jed reacted with the scorn reserved by small boys for their imbecilic mothers. "Only the most awesome woman in the world." He returned his attention to Marsha. "It's so cool you know her, Aunt Marsha."

"Can we meet her?" Will got straight to the point, as usual.

"You'll be sharing the house with her."

"No way!" the boys gasped in astonished unison.

"She's filming in this very bay for the next two weeks," Marsha said. "And I'm not letting her sleep in a trailer when we only live half a mile up the beach."

Jed and Will stared, slack-jawed, at the scene before them. The famous Gin Ito, doing stunts right here under their noses. Staying at their aunts' home. Obviously this was huge.

"Yup." Marsha read their faces with amusement. "They're filming *Red Revenge 2* here. And," she produced the ace card that would make her the coolest living family member *ever* in the boys' eyes, "I've got the job of doubling for Kelly Rose."

"Kelly Rose?" Solley felt painfully out of the loop. She recalled a particularly busty actress who starred in lame chick flicks. "Will she be here, too?"

"Well, not actually in the flesh," Janie said. "But you'll have a representation of her. Namely my beloved in a stuffed bra and big blond wig leaping about on a Jet Ski." She gave Marsha a teasing look. "Kelly will be shooting down at the studios while all the aqua-stunts are filmed on location, here at La Sirena Verde."

"Cool," Jed breathed. "This is gonna be the best vacation ever."

So much for peace and quiet, Solley thought. But at least the kids would be kept entertained, even if it wasn't in the way she'd imagined. "Janie, you should have said you had other guests. We could have come anytime in the next few weeks. I feel terrible that we're cramping you."

"No, you're not. We wanted you and the kids here more than ever. There's plenty of room for all." Janie plunked herself down on another huge towel a couple of feet away.

"Okay, if you're sure."

"You're my sister. Enough said."

They both watched Marsha and the kids wander away

along the sun-drenched beach toward the small crane Solley had seen erected earlier that morning. It stood sentinel over the movie camp that had sprouted from the dunes in mere hours and would be the home of the film crew for the next few weeks.

"How come Marsha's back in the saddle, so to speak?" she asked.

"Gin got her onboard. She suggested this place to the director as a good locale for the open-shot stunt scenes. I think she was kinda hoping Marsha's name would pop into his mind for a few of the aqua-stunts. Then she landed the stunt coordinator's job as well as stunt lead, so she put Marsha forward for the Jet Ski stuff."

"Do you think Marsha wants to get back into stunts full time?"

Janie and her partner were well into their sixth year of togetherness, and it crossed Solley's mind that Marsha might be expressing her upcoming seven-year itch by revisiting her daredevil roots. She and Janie had met on a movie set, much like the one farther down the beach. At the time, Janie was working as a computer consultant in special effects. Marsha Bren, as stuntwoman, was the fall guy for every female member of cast. Off script, she fell for Janie, and for her, love seemed to be a bottomless pit. Solley couldn't imagine how that worked. In her experience, falling in love meant the ground rushed up to meet her far too soon, threatening to smash her into a million pieces.

"God, I hope she isn't tempted to get back into that lifestyle." Janie's blond brows drew together. "I used to hate her forever traveling all over the world. I didn't get to see her for months on end. And then she would suddenly reappear, black and blue and aching all over, looking for love and attention and endless massages."

"I remember." Solley used to wonder what it must be like to have such an exciting life. Bringing up three children, more or less single-handedly, had anesthetized any desire for unexpected excitement. She needed order and stability. And support, a little support, would be a novelty.

"She's psyched at getting this job, of course," Janie mused. "It's been ages since she did any stunt stuff and she misses the thrill, but for the moment she's enjoying the steady studio work. Personal training pays well, and we're planning some changes so I need her close by."

"What changes?" Solley fully expected her sister to reel off a list of improvements to her already fabulous home. "Perhaps a helipad, servants' quarters, or maybe an east wing?"

Although she jibed, she was proud of her younger sister's successes. Janie was a shrewd businesswoman and a hard worker, and had done well for herself. Sometimes it was hard to believe they were sisters. They were quite different, physically. Solley was flame-haired and tall at 5'9", while Janie was a petite, vibrant blonde. They'd each inherited stunning green eyes and a quick-fire temper from their much-missed Irish mother. Solley would have been the first to admit that Janie had grabbed all the gray matter. She'd built a solid career and now had a small but strategic consultancy business of her own. A handful of lucrative contracts had helped her acquire the comfortable lifestyle she shared with Marsha.

Janie's wise choices and successes contrasted sharply against the battered backdrop of Solley's achievements. She worked in an office part time, preferring to be home after school for the kids, and her marriage was not so much on the rocks as sunk without trace. Solley didn't resent Janie's solid relationship and professional success. In fact, her sister's contentment and security gave her hope that good things were possible, that happiness and love and companionship could be found, if not now then perhaps at some future time. In Solley's world of cinders and broken hearts, Janie's happy-ever-after fairytale was the life the forlorn-yet-hopeful dream of.

"Come on," she prompted. "What are you planning now?"

Janie's eyes danced. "How about a nursery."

"You're planning a baby?" Solley felt a slow smile of delight opening up her face.

"Yes," Janie admitted somewhat shyly. "It's something we both want, and it seems like the time is right. Well, as right as it can be, I suppose."

"Oh, Janie, I can't think of a better home improvement." Solley leaned into her and gave her a huge, warm hug. "I'm so happy for you both. You'll be wonderful parents. And my kids will have a little cousin to grow up with."

"The studio gave us a pretty lucrative deal for using our land, so we can afford for me to take a year out and get knocked up." Janie smiled ruefully. "Of course, the other payoff is that Marsha gets a last fling throwing herself off moving objects for loads of hard cash before nesting with me for all eternity."

"Well, this is the perfect nest," Solley said. "I'm so delighted, sweetheart."

Janie owned La Sirena Verde, the private beach on Topaz Bay, where the film crew had set up camp. Solley was glad Marsha's studio connections had bought them the opportunity to plan for a family. Janie was right, there couldn't be a better time or place. Solley sighed and gazed out into the bay. Gulls swooped and soared idly in the lazy heat of the late afternoon, their haunting cries carried away on the wind. The peace and tranquility of the area raised her hopes for the quiet respite she so desperately needed.

I'm doing the right thing, she told herself for the umpteenth time. The kids needed this break away from the fighting between her and her partner, Danielle. Sinking back onto her beach towel, she let her mind clear and tried to concentrate on her innermost feelings. Slowly she felt her body relax, the tightness in her face and shoulders gradually melting away with the soothing ocean sounds. Beyond the love of her children and the comfort of her sister's home, she reached out timorously to touch the ever-present core of fear and sadness deep within. At the end of her long journey to this time and place, she was still an unloved, lonely woman.

Dan, you're such an ass. I don't want to start over with someone new. I'm too old to start over. I wish we could work this out. I wish you'd try harder for the kids' sake.

Solley hated the emotional mugging her kids were going through, but she was powerless to change the chain of events that had led to the current crisis. A parental split was harsh for children, no matter what age they were. Sadness clouded her gaze as she thought of her children's confusion. Jed, at eight years, was outgoing and boisterous. He excelled at sports, so he was popular at school and had no shortage of friends and adventures. Yet he always had time for his little brother and sister and was fiercely protective of them.

Will was six and much quieter. He might have been shyer, socially, but he was just as gifted at sports as his brother, especially in swimming. He could move through the water like a baby otter. He was a very loving child but, being naturally reserved, he seemed to quietly observe the interactions of his family instead of taking center stage. That role unquestionably belonged to his twin, Della, who was bright and artistic and currently passionate about anything pink. A baby diva waiting to explode, she had Will and Jed wrapped around her little finger. Solley privately felt sorry for the objects of her daughter's future affections. Having Della's attention was like being hit by a truck, then reversed over, only Della showed less mercy.

Drowsily watching the white surf break onto the shore, she hoped the vacation at La Sirena Verde would give the children a summer to remember for happier reasons than their parents splitting up.

❖

"So, tell me about Gin Ito," Solley asked a few hours later as she and Janie sliced celery and cucumber for a dinner salad. "I have no real idea who she is. Does that make me as lame as Jed and Will seem to think?"

"No, staying all those years with Dan makes you lame."

"Cheap shot."

"Well, you really go all the way down when you go slumming, don't you?"

"Considering she's an ex of yours, isn't that a bit rich?" Solley shot back, riled.

"Yeah, but I chose Marsha. I saw Dan for what she was and I warned you over and over. Crazy that two cousins could be so different."

"So, you've finally been proved right. Good for you, sis. Congratulations. My relationship is the crock of crud you always predicted. That's some set of crystal balls you got there." Solley turned toward the kitchen door, but Janie caught her arm.

"Look, I'm sorry. I just hate to see you hurting."

"Please, let's just drop it. I'm well aware of your opinion. I pulled the short straw, okay? Can we change the subject? It's getting old."

"Okay, I'll tell you everything about Gin Ito. How's that?"

"I can hardly wait." Why not discuss another high-achieving woman? Could she feel any worse about herself?

"She's Japanese American, and she's Marsha's best friend. They go way, way back, almost Jurassic…by that I mean college. I bet you've probably seen Gin in more movies than Kelly Rose."

"I don't think so." Solley had trouble noticing anyone else who starred alongside Kelly Rose's breasts.

"I know the name doesn't mean anything to you, but nearly every female stunt scene you've witnessed on screen in the past seven years or so probably starred Gin or she directed. She's the hottest stunt practitioner and engineer around."

"God, what a strange career choice."

"Imagine what I had to live with until my big beefcake came to her senses, under my subtle direction of course. She'd be a pancake at the bottom of a cliff by now if it wasn't for me—Ms. Floats Like a Butterfly, Drowns Like a Bee. I saved her life. That's why I own her."

They both smiled, then looked up at the crunch of tires on the gravel driveway out front. A few seconds later, footsteps crossed the deck at the rear of the house, moving toward the kitchen door.

"Hey, Janie." A warm voice carried through the open doorway into the shadowy kitchen. A slim figure, framed in sunlight, stood poised on the threshold.

"Talk of the sweet devil. You got here in double time." Janie wiped off her hands and rushed to hug the new arrival. "Marsha's down at your trailer waiting for you."

"I really need a shower, and if I went down there first, I'd get caught up in conversation with the crew and never get away." A dark, piercing gaze spilled past Janie to Solley, and the new arrival gave a charming grin. "Hi. Don't tell me, Janie's sister?"

"Sorry." Janie sidestepped. "Yes, this is Solley."

"Hi, Solley. I've heard a lot about you." Gin reached out her hand.

Solley was pleasantly surprised at the warm, solid handshake from the light grasp. "Ditto. My kids have been raving about you since we arrived and they found out you'd be filming locally."

Gin was not what she had expected of a famous stunt artist. Not that she was sure what to expect, but she'd assumed a big, strapping Amazon like Marsha, not the compact woman now before her. Gin was closer in height to Janie, around five feet two. Otherwise they were total opposites, one with short, inky hair and almond eyes the color of midnight, the other a honeyed blonde. With her height advantage, auburn hair, and freckles, Solley felt about as dainty as a giant redwood standing beside them.

Gin's well-honed body vibrated with health and vitality, almost in contrast to the stillness of her demeanor. Her eyes, swimming with sunlight, flicked to Solley before quickly darting away as if Gin felt self-conscious. Solley could swear there was a glint of happy mischievousness in their depths, and she felt herself warm to this woman immediately. Positive energy seemed to flow off her in waves. Solley had actually felt an electric tingle all over her body when their hands touched.

I must have some static in the attic, she mused to herself, surprised at her physical reaction to the handshake. Perhaps her poor mind was cracking under the stress of her situation. As Gin hoisted her heavy sports bag onto her shoulder in one easy move, muscles rippled up her arm and torso. *Lordy, somebody works out.* Solley blinked, slightly shocked at the lusty thoughts that suddenly buzzed through her mind.

"Sol and the kids are here for a few weeks' vacation," Janie explained. "And believe me, you couldn't have a more solid fan base than those little tykes. It'll be like residing at a fan convention for the next few weeks, you'll be so adored."

"Then I'd better get cleaned up. I smell far from adorable. Sea salt and sweat are not the best of colognes. It's one of the downsides of plummeting into the ocean twenty times in a row." Gin smiled directly at Solley and her shy reserve seemed to melt away. "But I'd love to meet your kids."

Solley smiled back. "They're dying to meet you. Thank you for being so kind, I'm sure you're exhausted after all that…plummeting."

"You're in the guest suite at the front," Janie told Gin. "Go grab a quick shower before Marsha and the kids get back."

"Yes, prepare to have your peace and tranquility forever shattered," Solley said dryly.

"Oh, and to keep things really restful we've got a red setter pup," Janie added cheerfully. "He's called Nelson and he's as dumb as driftwood. I think he's Marsha's totem animal." She rolled her eyes.

With a parting grin, Gin moved toward the back stairwell, obviously very familiar with the layout of the Rayner-Bren home. Solley was amazed that she'd never met Gin or even heard her name mentioned. Apparently they were both regular guests, even if Solley didn't manage to visit as often as she had in the past. She suppressed the suspicious thought that her sister had deliberately kept this old friend of Marsha's in a separate sphere. What did she imagine—that Gin wouldn't be safe around an unhappy, frustrated Rayner woman?

An elbow landed in Solley's ribs. "You're totally checking out her butt."

"I am not."

Janie slapped a cucumber into Solley's hand. "Here, think about something else."

Solley stared down at the long, hard vegetable and blinked. *I can't believe I'm ogling my sister's houseguest and eroticizing a salad item. Is this what my sex life has finally come to?*

❖

The moon hung low and the shore was quiet as Gin and Marsha wandered along the receding waterline.

"I really want this job to be my last," Gin said.

"I know, I know. You're getting old, Grandma. You need to retire so you can spend all those millions."

"Hey, I'm four months younger than you, Granny-pants."

"Granny-pants! You sure know how to hurt a girl. Cuts right to the heart."

They both giggled.

"Well, one day Junior will grow up and make you and Janie grandmas. I think it's obligatory to wear the panties. Right up to here." Gin indicated her armpits.

"Junior." Marsha savored the word. "Junior M. That sounds about right. Did you ever think you'd see the day I'd be a mommy?"

Gin's eyes shone with affection. "I can easily see the day. And I wish you joy. Janie is a beautiful person. I couldn't wish you anything better in life than a partner like her and the hope of a family."

"Not too sure if she'll go with the Junior M moniker, though." Marsha got a warm one-armed hug in response. Glancing sideways at Gin, she said cautiously, "I know this must be strange for you—"

"No, not at all. Life goes on and I must find my place in it. I've done my grieving and I really want to move out from under this cloud of depression. I'm desperate for a fresh start,"

Gin said. "When I see you and Janie…the happiness in others, I know I'm ready for it, too."

Her expression was earnest yet vulnerable, as if she knew the remedy but not the ingredients. They strolled on for a few more paces before Marsha broke the silence with a lighter topic. "Solley's kids sure can't get enough of you."

"She's nice and they're great kids. You'll have your work cut out for you if Junior M is a chip off the Rayner block."

Marsha smiled. "I love Sol and her little monsters. It's hard for them with the breakup and everything." She shrugged disconsolately. "It's gonna get messy. Dan's new girlfriend seems keen on grabbing the kids. Knowing Dan, it'll be a low-down and dirty fight."

"That sounds harsh."

"Yeah, it's such a fuckup. Sol doesn't care about alimony, or the house, or anything. Just the kids." Marsha gazed up at the starlit night. "She's a good mom. I wish she'd find someone special."

Stargazing and inner contemplation never took up too much of Marsha's time. Just as suddenly as she'd stopped to admire the heavens, she turned to Gin, buzzing with new energy, her thoughts sparking off in a million directions.

"Let's head back and you can tell me some more about this stunt school idea of yours. I might have a little money and whole lot of time to invest in a project like that."

CHAPTER TWO

Where are the kids?" Solley asked, finding Janie alone in the kitchen the following morning. Drawn by the aroma of fresh coffee, she poured a cup and sat down at the table.

"Marsha and Gin have taken them down to the camp for a walkabout. I thought a sleep-in would do you no harm."

"Oh." Solley wasn't sure how to take this. It was a rare experience to have another adult take charge of her kids, and for them to go so readily.

Janie reached over for her hand. "It's just to let you have a little time to yourself, as well. You can't always be hiding your emotions behind caring for others."

"I don't. And anyway, they're kids. They can't cope the way adults can."

"Sol, you need to survive this, too, not just shepherd the kids through it. What would happen to them if you fell apart?"

"Janie, I'm fine. It's not like it's a sudden shock. I've been dealing with the fallout for nearly five years, although I have to admit having the 'other woman' become a permanent fixture was a nasty surprise." In the past, Dan usually treated her flings like takeout food, discarding them once she'd had her fill. Solley was stunned that the latest, Trixie, had somehow inspired new rules.

"Dan's an unfaithful, thoughtless jerk." Janie said.

Solley sighed. "Please, don't start."

Janie held up both hands defensively. "I'm sorry. Discussion closed. I guess I'm just angry that she's throwing so much away. What an idiot."

"Her or me?"

Solley was tired of the topic. She'd come away to escape the self-recriminating voices in her head, not to have Janie replace them. Yes, she'd been idiotic to hang in there for so long. But there was a lot more than her ego at stake when it came to walking out the door. They were a family. And the truth was, Dan had a way of rescuing them at the last minute, of knowing when she'd pushed too far. Their relationship moved like the tide, ebbing and flowing with each heartbeat.

Until the day Dan ran out of caring and stopped trying to save them.

Now Solley had to rescue herself and the three little people who counted on her. "I just worry for the kids. I want this to be a special holiday full of fun and laughter."

"Trust me, they'll have an absolute ball with Gin."

Yeah, but I wanted it to be with me. Solley felt ashamed that the thought had jumped into her head. "Maybe I'll wander on down and catch up with them. Want to join me?"

"Nah, I'm in the study researching AI clinics. Gotta pick the best gravy for this little pot roast." Janie patted her flat belly. "Marsha wants us to choose a donor we know, but I want to check out alternatives before we decide."

"Sounds like a plan." Solley dropped a kiss on Janie's cheek. "See you later, sis."

She ambled away from the house and down the dunes and into the small village of trailers. The area heaved with frantic comings and goings as people prepared for the day's shoot. The random confusion of noise and motion made Solley fret. This seemed a dangerous environment for the kids to hang out in without her supervision. She needed to find Gin's trailer and rescue her family.

She checked doors as she wandered around the site. Some were labeled with names and others with their technical functions, like "Makeup," "Communications," and "Wardrobe." Turning a corner, Solley saw two young women, obviously part of the studio crew, emerge from one of the larger mobiles. They walked a little ahead, ignoring her, deep in conversation.

"Well, she's not at her love shack," said one.

"She's staying at that big house along the beach, with Marsha Bren and her lesbian lover. Apparently she's a frequent visitor."

"Oh, God. A threesome? I'd love to help even out those odds."

Both women snickered.

"She's so fit I bet she can fuck for days without coming up for air."

"If she was fucking me for days I'd be coming up for CPR."

"Yeah, it wouldn't be sex, it'd be murder."

"More like suicide. No, wait. Fuckicide. 'Cos you asked for it."

"Nah, it'd be fuckinasia, 'cos I begged for it."

They dissolved into snorts, leaving Solley in shock. Good grief, Gin seemed to have a fan base for *everything* she did. She eyed the trailer they'd emerged from. Gin Ito's name was on the door plaque. Those little gossips had probably been in there drooling over her used bed linen. Tempted to have a quick peek inside, she started toward the steps when she heard

Jed's voice and turned around. All three of her children were strolling toward her with Gin tagging behind, hand in hand with Della.

"Hey, guys." Solley smiled. "You all got up and out early this morning. I missed you."

Jed bounced up full of excitement. "Gin and Marsha took us to see around the movie camp. And Aunt Marsha showed us her Jet Ski. She's going to jump off it later."

"Where is Marsha?" asked Solley, conscious that Gin had sole adult responsibility for her kids. *Brilliant, my kids are running wild around the Circus Macabre with Ms. Death Fuck as a chaperone.*

"She's over at the jetty with the technicians," Gin replied. "She said she'd catch up with us for lunch."

"It's okay. I'll just take the kids back to the house and let you get some work done."

"Aw, Mom," wailed Jed. "Gin was gonna show us round her trailer. Let us see all her neat gear and stuff."

"Mmn." Solley was concerned at exactly what "neat gear and stuff" might actually be lying around the "love shack." Items of sexual torture and fuckicide had better have been tidied away.

"It's really no trouble," Gin said. "I enjoy their company. It's fun showing them around."

"We were gonna see all Gin's movie clothes and makeup and stuff." Will piped up. He sounded desperately disappointed.

"Pleeeze, let us stay. We'll be really, really good!" Della bleated alongside her brothers.

Great, make me look like Attila the Mom. Solley scowled inwardly. Outwardly she conceded, "Okay, half an hour, then. And you guys be good."

With a polite smile for Gin and a wag of her finger at her kids, she left the camp and trudged back the way she'd come.

So what was that all about? *Yet again I've been abandoned for a slinkier sports model.* First Dan and her new bimbo, and now the kids with their puppy eyes for Gin. Solley looked down at her rounded curves and sighed. Who was she kidding? After three kids, she was no sports model, more like a beat-up old people mover.

❖

Later that afternoon Solley, Janie, and the kids wandered down to the old jetty to watch from a distance as Marsha went through her paces for the Jet Ski scene.

"So what's going on?" Solley asked.

"Apparently Dufus is going to dive off a hurtling Jet Ski as a harpoon whizzes inches from her ears," Janie replied. "Meanwhile, back at the studio, Kelly Rose will be gently lowered into a tank of lovingly warmed water where she will wallow for the close-ups. She's no fool."

"Ah. So that would make you Mrs. Dufus, then."

Solley was rewarded with a glower. "As long as it's not Widow Dufus, I'll cope."

Shielding her eyes, Solley gazed across the water. Marsha was zipping crazily about, her blond wig whipping in the wind, the foamy spray splashing up around her silver and hot pink wet suit. A black speedboat buzzed around her loaded with three ominous figures, obviously the bad-guy actors in this scene. One was pointing a harpoon gun at the spinning Jet Ski. Two other rescue speedboats stayed a decent distance to port and starboard, out of camera range.

"They're not actually going to shoot at her?" Solley squeaked with alarm.

Two other larger vessels, armed with cameras, added to the crazed mix of zooming craft out in the bay. As the kids yelled and hooted like barbarians, the Jet Ski soared about five feet into the air, the pink figure jettisoning skyward, spinning around the flying harpoon and diving down into the sea.

"Oh, my God," blurted Solley.

"Is it safe to look?" Janie squinted from behind her fingers.

The scene was quickly reassembled and the crazy wheeling started all over again. And so the afternoon wore on until the pattern suddenly changed. This time Marsha spun awkwardly into the water and one of the accompanying speedboats cut quickly across to the abandoned Jet Ski.

"What's going on?" Solley asked as her silent children gazed intently at the unfolding scene.

Engines were cut and shouts rose from various craft.

Janie's face was waxen. "Something's wrong."

Solley clutched her around the shoulders as a rescue boat turned and plowed toward the scene, sending spray high on either side. A dark figure dived from its deck.

"That's Gin!" shouted Jed. "She'll save Aunt Marsha."

❖

Too late, Gin had noticed the rogue wave from the corner of her eye as it bellied obliquely across the bay to rise in a vicious crest toward the Jet Ski. Marsha, already on the upward rise, had no chance of correcting her tilt. Before Gin could raise a warning cry, her friend had been broached and was flung up and over, her practiced trajectory in shambles with no room for correction. At last finding her voice, Gin had howled an alarm before launching herself from the moving rescue craft.

A few firm strokes brought her alongside Marsha's semiconscious form. The waves were high, banging into them. Gin floated on her back, Marsha cradled between her legs. She struggled to keep them both buoyant, nursing her best friend's head and shoulders above the water until they were heaved into a rescue boat.

Stunt crews had their own medics on standby for events such as this, and by the time the vessel reached the pier, the area was a heaving mass of orchestrated activity. Marsha, now conscious and upright, sat beside Gin, who had a comforting arm around her. The studio paramedics dashed onto the boat to attend to Marsha's left leg and check her for concussion.

Gin leapt onto the jetty to meet Janie, who had descended on the scene with the rest of her family following anxiously behind.

"Janie, it's okay," she said. "She was only out for a split-second and didn't inhale any water. She's gashed her leg. It's bleeding but I don't think it's a break. The paramedics will take her to the hospital once they get her strapped up."

"I'll break more than her damn leg," Janie snapped. "Let me through."

She stepped gingerly into the boat, reaching for her extremely pale partner. Janie's bravado bubble burst immediately and tears began spilling down her face. Marsha wrapped her in a protective embrace, pulling her into her broad shoulder. They snuggled close as the medics sutured and bandaged the cut leg and swollen ankle.

Cupping Janie's damp cheek in her palm, locking her gaze lovingly with the tearful green eyes before her, Marsha whispered, "Don't worry, babe." The injured now the comforter, she added, "Just a bad day at the office, that's all."

❖

"What's the verdict?" Solley asked several hours later when the walking wounded finally returned from the hospital.

Marsha limped between Janie and Gin, her two minders,

her smile a complete contrast to their anxious faces. "Well, I have eighteen stitches on the shin and a mighty big bang on my lucky ankle. It's weakened from two earlier breaks. I'm always spraining and straining it, so no biggie, just crap timing."

"And this would be your lucky ankle…why?"

"Because it's not my other ankle. That one is still good. Unbroken, see? Virgin bones."

Janie, following behind, rolled her eyes at these words of wisdom. "Virgin brain, more like," she muttered.

They limped inside, leaving Solley and Gin alone in the warm breeze blowing in from the bay. Taking a seat on the deck steps, they looked out across the water, neither making the kind of small talk these occasions seemed to call for.

After a while, Solley broke the companionable silence. "Would you like a cold beer?"

"That would be lovely."

"It was a good job you were there today." Solley returned after a few moments and passed Gin the newly opened bottle.

"I could tell the minute the wave hit the Jet Ski that she wasn't going to pull out of the angle of tilt correctly," Gin said. "It's a hazard with aqua-stunts. The conditions have no consistency. Every run rewrites the rules of the previous one."

She took a long draw from her bottle, and Solley watched her throat work as she swallowed the cool beer. She, too, found herself swallowing as the moonlight played on the angular planes of Gin's face and the muscles moving under the smooth skin of jaw and throat.

She was gorgeous. Solley could hardly blame the kids for wanting to run away with her at every opportunity. Shit, half the film crew wanted to run away with her, if not commit fuckicide in her bed.

"I like your kids." Gin turned to her. "They're really great, and loads of fun. Della has an answer for everything."

Flustered at being caught red-handed examining the other woman's profile, Solley replied, "Yeah, she's certainly the alpha bitch in that little cub pack. I'm glad they seem to be having so much fun here. God knows, things are hard enough at home for them."

"I'm sorry about that," Gin said cautiously.

Solley sensed she was open to more personal disclosures, and maybe one day they would have that kind of conversation. If Solley could ever stand to think about her life, let alone discuss it with a stunning, successful woman like the one in front of her. Wanting to stick to safe superficialities, she said, "Meeting you was the icing on a very big holiday cake. But please don't let them run you ragged. We all know you're here to work."

"Hey, I'm more than pleased to see them in my free time."

Wow, how could someone so sweet also burn holes in the sheets? Solley cleared her throat, embarrassed at her intimate thoughts and feeling a sudden need for more self-control in this woman's quiet, yet unsettling presence. "Janie tells me Marsha and you are old friends."

"Yeah, we've known each other forever. She has a real big heart. I'm glad she met your sister. It turned her life around."

"They're a great couple. I love visiting with them."

"Me, too," Gin said. "They're always so happy. It gives one hope."

"What about you? Do you have someone special somewhere?" Solley winced at blurting out such an awkward, intrusive question.

Gin's smile was bittersweet. She seemed lost in a loving

memory for several seconds. "Not at the moment." Her smile seemed to falter slightly. "I'm too busy running all around the world to be meeting those 'special someones.' The movie industry is very shallow, with more takers than givers. And it's hard to meet people from outside it, so for the time being I prefer not to get involved." Her dark eyes settled on Solley. "But life goes on and things change."

Unsure how to respond, Solley said, "Oh. Well, you're probably very wise to be careful. But I'm glad things are shifting for you. It's good to open up to life's possibilities."

Listen to yourself, you big procrastinator. Go preach it from the mountain. Fake!

"Sometimes," Gin agreed. "Then again, there are times we all need to be alone just to think and reassess. I find La Sirena Verde the perfect place to do that. When I'm not throwing myself all over it, that is."

"Mmn, you do plummet beautifully." Solley grinned.

"That's another thing I need to think about. We've a saying, that old bones don't bounce. I'm getting too long in the tooth for this caper. Unlike Marsha, I'm not sure if I have any virgin bones left, and I'm beginning to feel it in the cold weather."

Her grin became mischievous, almost on the verge of flirtatious, but not quite. Solley's heart lurched into an odd dysrhythmia.

"I'm beginning to see damage sort of comes with the paycheck," she remarked.

"After today, I don't think Janie wants that sort of money anymore," Gin said. "And she's right. If they're going to start a family and snuggle down into this fine feathered nest they've made for themselves, it would be crazy for Marsha to get back into stunt work. La Sirena Verde is a lovely place for a real life, doing what matters."

She reached for her empty beer bottle at the same time Solley moved to collect it. Once again, as their hands brushed, Solley got a rush of goose bumps along her arm. It made her heart do giddy, teenage things, and much to her embarrassment, her cheeks flushed. *Oh please, Rayner, what's with the hormone surge?* Next thing she'd be getting pimples like an overgrown, gawky teenager.

Flustered by her body's heated betrayal, she collected the empty bottles and quickly rose. "Well, I better get to bed. Thanks for the company and the chat. I'll see you in the morning."

"Good night," Gin responded, picking up on Solley's discomfort.

The stiffness in her voice and her body suggested a line that couldn't be crossed, and Gin mentally kicked herself for her insensitivity. Way to go. The woman's home was falling apart and Gin had to remind her of other people's happiness. Klutz.

She sat for a few moments musing about the battered little family she was just beginning to get to know. The kids were real gems, funny and intelligent and great company. Just being in their presence gave her a boost she needed. Their mother was a very attractive woman, but plainly tired and stressed and carrying a great deal of pain. Gin's heart went out to her. Divorce was such a messy business, with so many innocent victims.

Marsha had mentioned a third party. Gin could only imagine what a fool this "Dan" was to walk away from a beautiful wife and fantastic kids, for another woman. It was sad that the real treasures in life were so seldom seen for what they were. The thought made her all too aware of her own emptiness. Despite her career success and money, she felt hollow, that she held no substance, only cobwebs to wrap around what looked from the outside to be a perfect life. There was nothing of true comfort to cradle her. She was spiritually and emotionally bereft and had no idea how to move through her current emotional impasse and make her life different.

Sighing, she shook the heavy, unwelcome feelings away. It had been a long and eventful day, but she'd made it through to the end. And thanks to Solley Rayner and her kids, she was looking forward to the rest of the week.

CHAPTER THREE

Marsha's woeful predicament became the children's endless fixation over the next two days. Her bruised, swollen foot stuck out from the knee-to-ankle bandaging like a black-and-blue horror film prop.

"Will you lose your toes?" Della asked on Thursday morning.

"Did you actually see your own bones?" Jed hovered, fascinated. "Gross," he said with approval.

"I like the color." Della considered the marbled bruising. "Purple is my new best favorite."

"Maybe you'll get gangrene," Jed enthused.

Will, looking on with a thoughtful expression, finally asked, "If a rat ate your foot when you were asleep, would you feel it?"

Janie came to the rescue with another dose of painkillers. "Right, my little ghouls, I'm off into town to collect Hopalong's next fix from the pharmacist. Who wants to come with me? Maybe we can stop at a toy shop and get some of those massive water guns, now that Aunt Marsha's a sitting duck?"

Janie leaned in to kiss her partner warmly before collecting the car keys and following the children out the door.

"I know you love her, but sometimes your sister's a little bastard," Marsha growled at Solley.

"Funnily enough, that's what mother used to say. Our baby sister is the real angel of the family." Solley smiled. Grace was twenty-four and in her third year at the USC School of Dentistry. "I can't believe she'll be qualified in another year. Imagine, a real live dentist in the Rayner family. Mom would be so proud."

"I don't know why you and Janie are so surprised. All that pain and discomfort…sounds like the perfect career choice for a Rayner sister."

"That's rich, coming from a woman whose career path has led her off a cliff top more than once."

Marsha shrugged. "Sol, if you don't have any plans for this morning, would you help me down to the jetty? Gin's replacing me for the last of the Jet Ski shots and I'd really like to be there."

"Sure, no problem." Solley's reply was slightly breathless.

She was curiously pleased at the thought of watching Gin in action again. In fact, being around her in any situation lifted Solley's spirits. The quiet focus and steady energy of the stuntwoman was addictive. Gin seemed to seek out Solley's company in the evenings, and it was comforting simply to sit with her and feel a connection.

With a start Solley realized that was exactly what was happening…she felt a connection. Not judged, or vulnerable, or pitied. Gin seemed to accept Solley's mess of a life for what it was, the nadir of hope and joy, where even falling into despair took too much effort. Solley sensed that she'd been there, too. She knew this journey. The realization intrigued her. Gin Ito intrigued her. *Hell, if misery loves company I could do a lot worse than sip beer with Gin Ito.*

And now that she had a rudimentary understanding of how the Jet Ski stunt was supposed to look, she might even be able to make intelligent comments about the performance.

❖

The jetty was a heaving mass of activity. All the seagoing vessels, including numerous trashed up Jet Skis, were moored alongside the weathered boards. A variety of sound, film, and techno people rushed through their work in choreographed motion.

As Solley and Marsha progressed along the moorings, the crowd parted and they beheld the wondrous sight of Gin idling astride a Jet Ski, clad in a lurid pink and platinum wetsuit and ridiculous blond wig.

Solley snorted down a laugh as she and Marsha stood at the edge looking down at her. "Oh, my God. You're like the Silver Surfer in drag."

The stuntwoman looked so colorfully plastic it was easy to imagine her as a parody of the sixties comic book superhero. She was all silicone and sassiness.

Gin glanced up through the long tendrils of her gaudy wig. Her dark eyes sparkled with mischief. "The jealousy's eating you up, isn't it?"

"And just where the hell did you get those from?" Marsha thrust a probing finger toward Gin's suddenly ample chest.

"Well, the truly scary thing," Gin deadpanned, "is that I'm meant to look like you looking like Kelly Rose looking like Red Revenge. So don't start on me about these tits. I take it you didn't need a stuffed bra."

Solley giggled at the spectacle of the slim woman bedecked with garish blond tresses and a chest that would land her flat on her face if she wasn't hanging onto the Jet Ski throttles. "And there I was thinking they were buoyancy aids."

"Oh, the world is so full of funny white women with big tits," Gin responded with a saucy smile. "Must be where you store all your humor."

"Boob envy. So common, so sad." Marsha sighed.

"It must be an enormous obstacle to overcome." Solley shook her head sadly.

"I hope we don't have a bust-up," Marsha continued.

"Impossible. Isn't she your *bosom* buddy?"

"Yes, and tit wouldn't be the same without her." They both collapsed in giggles at their atrocious jokes.

"Well, girls, thanks for the mammaries, but see ya later." Gin sniffed. Revving up the engine, she slowly pulled away from the pier.

Solley smiled at the sight of the buxom "superhero" bouncing over the waves with as much dignity as she could muster. The banter had lifted her spirits. She'd enjoyed the twinkle in Gin's eyes as they swapped terrible puns. She'd also noticed the way Gin's gaze drifted discreetly to her breasts. Normally Solley would recoil if she caught someone looking at her that way. But Gin's appraisal didn't seem salacious. If anything, it indicated a physical awareness Solley found herself responding to. Why else would she be standing here on this jetty, glued to every move of that lithe, tight body but not giving a damn about the stunt?

❖

Later, during the afternoon, Solley and her sister calmly prepared dinner in the kitchen while outside a gang war raged. Marsha, given her delicate condition, had ensconced herself upstairs on her bedroom balcony and proceeded to wreak revenge on the junior members of her family as a water-gun sniper. Meanwhile, Gin leaped and dived across the sand dunes in a series of ruthlessly executed guerrilla tactics, wielding her own "weapon" to leave a trail of waterlogged devastation. The kids were in hysterics, running from haphazard ambush to full-face confrontation. All were soaked beyond hope, but in the hazy heat of the late afternoon the air was warm and their energy remained high.

Once dinner was ready, Solley opened the kitchen door and moved out onto the soaked deck, waving the white napkin of peace to holler for a suppertime truce. It was not to be. A merciless arc of water whipped up from the dunes and hit her squarely on the chest. Spluttering in surprise, she heard Janie curse as more water flew past her through the open door and into the kitchen.

"Right, that's it," Solley commanded in her most enraged matriarchal tone. "Weapons down and get your squelchy asses onto this deck right now."

Recognizing her end-of-all-good-things voice, the kids trudged up to the deck, heads lowered, guns trailing, and bottom lips extruded.

"What were the rules?" Solley asked as they lined up before her.

"Gin did it," Della said.

"No excuses. Look at the kitchen floor. It's soaked." She broke off when the kids convulsed into fits of giggles, their eyes focused beyond her.

Turning around, she was speechless for several seconds. There, like a giant bat, hung Gin, suspended from the balcony by her feet and pulling faces behind Solley's back, much to the snorting glee of her children.

Eye to eye, in a weird upside-down way, Solley scolded, "Oh, and you must be the mature adult. And, by the way, thanks." She indicated her soaked T-shirt.

Gin's gaze followed her accusing finger. Solley glanced down, too, immediately blushing as she became aware of the thin semitranslucent material that clung to her hardened nipples, clearly outlining the raspberry contours. *Fuck, where did those come from?* Horrified that she'd drawn Gin's attention to… well, her attention-seeking nipples, she folded her arms across her chest. *Christ, why don't I just send her a pornographic picture of myself.*

After a slight hesitation, Gin tore her attention from the wet T-shirt. Throwing a quick glance at the children, she drew herself back up onto the balcony above, out of sight. The kids howled with laughter at the deliberate clowning.

Joining in the fun as much to cover her own embarrassment as to please the kids, Solley yelled, "Come down here right now, you little squirt. I want a word with you."

She headed for the stairs. No sooner had she moved in that direction than Gin vaulted over the balcony railings onto the deck. She landed like a silent assassin at the fringes of Solley's peripheral vision, indicating for the kids to be quiet as she attempted to sneak up.

Spinning around, Solley aimed a finger at her. "And don't think I don't see you."

She lunged halfheartedly at Gin and they launched into a quick, farcical circuit around the couch in the family room. Gin yipped and yahooed and Sol scolded, both hamming it up to the kids' delighted hoots of laughter. Their clowning continued until Solley caught her heel on the coffee table and lost her balance. The back of her knees hit the armrest of the couch and, falling backward, she grabbed for the front of Gin's top, dragging the smaller woman down with her onto the soft cushions.

They lay there nose to nose, and for a short, stunned moment Solley found herself sucked into the glowing depths of Gin's enigmatic eyes. She could feel the hard length of Gin's sinewy body pressing down on her, one steely thigh slowly pushing her softer ones apart.

Gin, supporting what little of her weight she could on

palms sunk deep into the plump cushions, could feel herself sliding closer and closer to the full petal lips that parted moistly below hers. So close they could share air, and still she was slipping uncontrollably closer. She could feel the heat pulsing from Solley's belly and smell the warm scent of her soft white throat. Solley's pebbled nipples scraped against Gin's chest.

"Are they making a baby?" Della's innocently perplexed voice cut through their overloaded senses.

"Dunno." Jed shrugged in disinterest.

Exchanging a horrified look over their predicament, the two women hastily scrambled to their feet. Solley patted her hair in place, looking everywhere but at Gin. Something shifted in her consciousness. She realized she had practically been flirting. Well, sort of flirting, which was okay considering she was so rusty. She cast a shy sideways glance at Gin and knew at once that she was flustered, too. Straightening her shirt, Gin fussed over her cuffs, her small ears glowing red with embarrassment. The soft pulse at the base of her throat throbbed, fascinating Solley with its fluttering dance until all she wanted to do was press her lips to it. The impulsive thought startled her. She smiled. It was nice to feel attraction toward another woman, even if only for one flashing, sultry moment.

Rather weakly, she ordered the children to go wash and change before dinner. Gin's eyes never left her, and Solley could read the unspoken question in their depths even though she doubted what she was seeing. She herded the kids out of the room. They were hungry so they didn't put up much resistance. She knew she should go after them, but she stayed and faced Gin.

"I'm sorry. That was more than a little embarrassing."

"They're only children. They enjoyed the game," Gin assured her softly.

Solley gave a firm nod. "Yes, that's all it was. Just harmless fun to cheer up the kids."

"Yes. I enjoyed it. You did, too, didn't you?"

Solley kept nodding. "Of course."

"Then maybe we can fool around again sometime." With a sly grin, Gin ducked out of the room, leaving a slightly stunned Solley in her wake.

Bemused, she flung herself back down onto the couch. What the hell? *Maybe we can fool around again...* The double meaning of Gin's parting shot played havoc with her senses. *God, you're one stupid horny bitch,* she remonstrated herself. *Stupid horny bitch?* Yes, and it felt good for a change. Solley was surprised. It felt safe and invigorating to think about flirting with Ms. Gin Ito. She hugged the feeling like a cozy little secret. She mentally patted her reawakening libido. *Welcome to the world, baby girl.*

Her heart raced, making it hard for her to stay put. She thought about finding Janie and Marsha and having a civilized adult evening, with wine and conversation after the kids went to bed, but all she really wanted was some alone time.

She collected a light shawl from her room and dropped by the kitchen on her way out. Doing her best to appear innocent and unshaken by the muddle of feelings Gin had stirred up, she said, "Hey. I'm not that hungry, Janie. Are you okay managing the kids if I skip dinner and go for a walk?"

"Sure, hon. I'll leave you some lasagna." Janie gave her a long look.

Solley escaped quickly and ambled down to the beach. She followed the shoreline, bare toes tickled by the bubbling surf and warm, wet sand. Up above, stars shone as cold and hard as diamonds, making her feel inconsequential and lost in the scheme of things and the passing of time.

"What the hell am I doing?" she whispered to the galaxies.

Hiding. The word looped in her mind, harsh in its truth. She'd always hidden. She hid behind the children while the love hemorrhaged out of her partner's heart. She was hiding at her sister's house as Dan consulted lawyers back home. She was even hiding out here on the beach, scared of what she might see if she looked in Gin Ito's eyes over dinner. And how she might feel.

"I'm useless at love and terrified of lust," she blurted to an unsympathetic ocean. "God, what a stupid cow. Where did all my courage go? When did that happen?"

It was true. She was a lioness where her children were concerned, but a coward when it came to facing her own needs. She thought back to the vibrant, fun-filled woman who had caught Dan's roving eye. How they had loved, madly, passionately. She was the one with fire enough to enslave her lover. And then what? Wedded bliss and Dan's infidelities, one after the next, chipping away at her confidence, tapping at her self-esteem like a million tiny blows of a sculptor's hammer until she was completely reshaped. Remodeled into this fabricated shell of a woman who hid on beaches because she was too scared to take a chance.

Shivering, she pulled her shawl around her tighter and took one more look at the heavens. She refused to live in this vacuum anymore, numbly going through the motions of each day. She was suffocating, and there was only one person with the power to change that. If she wanted to feel better, she would have to make it happen all by herself.

Facing the distant lights of Janie's house, she began her walk back, muttering a mantra as she went. "Tonight I'm starting over. What's done is done. Tomorrow I'll be braver."

CHAPTER FOUR

"G in Ito, I need to see you."

The furious bellow ripped apart Gin's solitary early morning tai chi. Peace, harmony, and inner equilibrium all popped like a bubble as she faced the tall, flame-haired Valkyrie striding across the sand toward her.

"What exactly did you tell my sister happened between us last night?"

"Nothing." Gin was amazed at how her heartbeat could drum in her head, the wind could howl in her ears, and her tongue could flap like a cat door. All because this very angry woman had descended on her like a raging, red sandstorm. "Nothing happened, so what could I possibly tell her?"

"Well, I can't answer that since I wasn't there. All I know is that someone gave her the impression we were making out."

Gin frowned as she joined the dots. She'd passed the door of the children's room last night as Janie and Marsha were putting them to bed. Pausing to take pleasure in the sweet family scene, she'd caught the tail end of a conversation about making babies. Her name and Solley's were mentioned in the mix, to her horror, and she'd fled before Janie and Marsha could tease her.

"I think the children squealed," she explained awkwardly.

"Obviously they misunderstood what they saw and said incorrect things to your sister."

"Let me get this right. My children squealed incorrect things?" Solley quoted, eye to eye with her quarry.

Gin squirmed. She felt like a big, fat stool pigeon, betraying the kids. More wind blew through the cat door. This conversation wasn't getting any easier. "I have a feeling they thought we were trying to make a baby."

"Make a baby?" Solley stared at her incredulously. "So this snippet of misinformation came to my sister's attention, and you knew it, but you did nothing to correct the impression? Would you care to elucidate?"

"I only overheard part of a conversation, then they saw me and I…ran away. Marsha was busting a gut laughing and Janie went sort of…evil."

"Janie's a bitch when she's got one over on someone. Been there, suffered that, forced to eat the T-shirt."

Gin wasn't sure if Solley was letting her off the hook or suggesting that she was a wimp. "I should have said something. I guess it just didn't occur to me that Janie would take it seriously. Or tease you, too."

Solley regarded her seriously. "She's my sister, and in case you didn't know Marsha is my partner's cousin. They talk."

"I thought you and your partner were breaking up." The words were out before Gin realized she'd been tactless and could have used a more neutral tone. But that was certainly Marsha's version of events.

"We're working through some problems." Solley's tone was defensive and cagey, discouraging further discussion. "Couples with children don't just break up. It's not that simple."

Gin didn't mention the other woman Marsha had talked

about. Who knew what really went on inside anyone else's relationship? Trying to respect Solley's privacy, she said, "I know this is a tough time for your family and that things are stressful. I don't want to cause a problem."

Solley sighed. "You're not the problem. I'm just saying, things are delicate at home and incidents like this can become ammunition against me."

Gin wanted to point out the double standard that seemed to be at work. Was she supposed to tiptoe around this woman and her children to spare the feelings of a cheating partner? Was Solley so invested in her relationship she couldn't see the irony in that?

"Sure. I understand." She met Solley's eyes. They were a calmer sea green now that the storm had passed.

After a long hesitation, Solley said, "We probably were a bit too...familiar or overenthusiastic with each other, or something. I can understand why Jed might have mistaken what he saw."

A sensible woman would agree and move on, but Gin gave in to an impulse. "Was he mistaken?"

Solley tensed visibly and her generous mouth tightened along with her voice. "Yes, he was." Her eyes dared Gin to challenge her.

Gin opted to defuse the rising tension. As though she hadn't noticed Solley's distinct unease, she said, "Hey, we're doing some reshoots this afternoon, just low-key stuff, nothing extreme." She placed a hand lightly on Solley's arm. "What say I take the kids with me? Give you some space. Let's call it an 'I'm sorry I didn't deal with this at the time' apology. Please?" Her dark eyes pleaded.

Solley felt herself soften. The heat from the hand on her arm traveled up to her tense shoulders and she relaxed a little under the pleasant tingle. "I guess I could finish a few errands."

"Yes, you could head into town. Do some shopping. Have lunch. Chill." Gin stopped talking, aware that she was almost babbling.

"Sounds good. But be careful, okay?" Solley's tone hardened. "No leaping, climbing, jumping, dangling, or other hazardous activities."

Relieved, Gin said, "Trust me, it'll just be a stroll. I promise."

❖

"Redheads really do have a bad temper," Gin observed as she sat at the kitchen table having a light lunch with Janie, Marsha, and the Rayner kids. She studied the white-blond mops of wind-crazed hair across from her, noting absently, "It's strange how all her children are incredibly blond."

"Let me explain," Janie said. "First of all, yes, she is an evil, bad-tempered bitch when she wants to be. Also, apparently redheads and brunettes always produce fair-haired children. It's a genetic thing."

Marsha and Gin both digested this interesting news while regarding the mopheads opposite.

"You mean someone dark like me would have blond kids with Solley?" Gin mused out loud.

Marsha obviously found the idea fascinating, while Janie paused, evidently tallying up the many things wrong with that statement.

"Again, let me explain," Janie said. "First of all, you are not a brunette, you have ink-black hair. Secondly, the genetic rule applies only to Caucasians, as far as I'm aware, and you're Asian. And last but not least, I don't think you could get my sister knocked up no matter how hard you tried. But if you do have the secret of parthenogenesis, please share it with Marsha as it would save us a small fortune and a lot of time."

Laughing, Gin said, "I wish."

"By the way." Marsha indicated Will's left eye. "Check out that bruise now."

Janie examined her nephew's face in consternation. "Those frozen peas were a big help."

They'd tried the improvised ice pack as soon as Gin walked in the door with the children half an hour earlier. Will wasn't the only casualty of their time together that morning. Jed had a sprained wrist from a fumbled jump off his aunts' balcony. The sprain was only minor, but Gin had bandaged it just in case. She didn't want Solley thinking she'd neglected her kids.

"I think we should put the patch back on him." Marsha produced the black pirate's patch Will had found in Gin's trailer. He'd insisted on wearing it all morning.

"Cool," he said, eagerly sliding it back over his injured eye. "Wait till Mom sees this."

"Indeed." Gin winced at the thought. So much for the sedate stroll she'd promised.

"Oh, you really are a grand example," Marsha drawled smugly.

"What are you talking about?"

"We've got Jed leaping about like a lemming, almost breaking bones. And Will tried to poke something into his eye."

"Also," Janie chimed in, "God only knows what weird shit these kids will be up to in later years after what they witnessed on the couch last night." She shook her head sagely. "They're at such a delicate age in their sociopsychological development, too."

"I can see I'll have to closely monitor your access to Junior M." Marsha tut-tutted.

"Who's Junior M?" Janie asked.

Marsha's eyes guiltily dropped to Janie's flat belly.

"Oh, I see." Janie snorted. "I can't even get you to look at an AI Web site, yet you've managed to name the baby? And you." She flashed her eyes in Gin's direction. "You're groping my sister and trying to mutilate my nephews. What kind of zoo do you think my house is?"

There was only one bona fide way out of this conversation. "I have an appointment," Gin said, jumping to her feet. "Gotta go."

"Oh, no, you don't." Janie gripped her wrist. "You're not leaving us to deal with her. When she sees those injuries, you're the one in the firing line, got that?"

"They're nothing," Gin protested.

"That's exactly what you can tell her," Marsha said cheerfully. "And I want front-row tickets."

"Oh, my God," Janie breathed in alarm as a vehicle approached the house. "You better steel yourself. This is not going to be pretty."

Gin craned so she could see out the window. Solley's Ford Escape slid to a halt and she jumped out and unloaded several bags of shopping. She looked so carefree, Gin wanted to rush out and distract her, anything to delay the inevitable. But before she could take a step, Will catapulted from his seat and out the kitchen door.

"Look at me, Mom. I'm a pirate," he yelled happily.

Not to be outdone, Jed charged after him, waving his bandaged wrist. "I nearly broke my arm."

Gin followed him as far as the door and physically winced at his shouted words. She threw a desperate look back to

Marsha, who was already trying to blend into the wallpaper. "She's going to kill me, isn't she?"

Marsha nodded a solemn affirmative. "Leave me all your money."

"What happened, sweetie?" Solley gathered Jed into a hug. She seemed completely relaxed, except for the laser beam look that unerringly picked out Gin, who was lurking in the shadow of the kitchen doorway.

"I was doing a stunt."

Gin swallowed hard. She could feel the blood draining from her face even as her feet drew her forward.

Solley stared suspiciously at Will's pirate's mask, then lifted the edge enough to reveal the huge bruise. "How did you hurt yourself?"

"I don't know." Will pulled away from her. "Did you get ice cream?"

"Yes." Solley fixed her gaze on Gin. "Why is my child half blinded?"

"Well," Gin began awkwardly, "he was in my trailer…and he somehow managed to stab himself with a mascara brush. I mean, it's a lot less than it looks. It stung a little bit, but the doc washed it out and put some drops in. He said the bruising came from Will rubbing his eye too hard. The patch was more to placate him than anything, really."

"A mascara brush," Solley repeated flatly.

"I think he's got a movie makeover thing going on. He really loves the patch." Gin could hear herself making feeble excuses and could see how unimpressed Solley was. Adopting a different tack, she said, "Look, I'm sorry. I think I'm cursed around your kids."

"And Jed?"

"We all know how mad Jed is about stunts." Janie emerged

from behind Gin. "None of us thought he'd play Tarzan from the upper floor. You can't blame Gin for that. He could just as easily have copied some of the mad stuff Marsha does."

"I've been bringing him here since he was a baby and that hasn't happened."

"You're right." Gin tried groveling, since explaining herself wasn't working. "I take complete responsibility."

"I suppose we can only be thankful that you didn't decide to immolate yourself," Solley said, unmoved. "Or stick your head in a blender. Perhaps if you had merely gargled with bleach…"

Gin could see the brooding storm in Solley's eyes and thought a tactful retreat best, but each biting word seemed to nail her to the ground. There was nothing she could do here except grab a shovel from Janie, so she could dig a hole where her remains could be buried in the sand later.

"This is meant to be a relaxing family holiday," Solley snapped. "Dan's going to freak if I bring the kids back looking like they've done a tour with the Marines."

"I'm so sorry. It never occurred to me he would copy the balcony leap."

"If you knew anything about children, you'd realize what should 'never occur' most definitely will," Solley lectured.

Gin lowered her eyes as a flash of pain made her wince. The words really stung. Solley had no idea how much, and Gin wasn't going to tell her. The loss of her son was still too painful to put into words. Behind her, Janie couldn't find a coherent sentence either. Only a few strangled squeaks emerged.

Solley looked appalled with both of them. "It seems I'm the one cursed with you around my kids, Gin. Obviously you won't be happy until we're all lifted out of here by air ambulance. Thank you *so* much for the relaxing afternoon."

She shoved past Gin and Janie and dumped her purchases on the kitchen counter.

"Solley, wait." Janie rushed after her. "You're making too much of this. They're kids, and they're just having fun. Boo-boos happen."

Solley spun round, face pale, green eyes livid. "You know as well as I do what Dan's planning. I'm not going to lose my children over *her*." She pointed at Gin.

Gin sucked her breath sharply, momentarily winded by the accusation. "I would never do—"

"But you already did. You promised to look after them and I come back to find them black and blue? I'm in a custody battle here. Dan's trying to take the kids away from me. And I won't lose them…I can't lose them." Her fears put a harsh edge to her voice. As though she knew she was exposing too much raw emotion, too much of her inner self, she struggled visibly to rein in her temper. "They're everything to me. I'm not going to lose them over your negligence."

Stricken, Gin could only watch helplessly as Solley walked out.

❖

Gin slowly mounted the veranda steps. She'd worked late over last-minute rushes, glad of the diversion from Solley's brooding silence and her own guilt that she had caused anxiety to someone who already had plenty to cope with. Gin totally understood Solley's stress levels concerning her kids, given a nasty divorce and custody battle pending. She would have been even more careful if she'd known the facts.

Hearing voices on the back deck, she ambled along the sun-baked redwood boards to the rear of the house. A quick glance in the open kitchen door brought her to a halt. Solley stood in the shadowy interior, bent over the open oven, inspecting what smelled like a tray of cookies. Her emerald swimsuit was covered by a T-shirt that rode up over her bottom, revealing an expanse of long, tanned legs.

Nice calves. Gin observed the musculature with a professional eye. Nice hamstrings and glutes, too. Her gaze traveled across the toned skin to the intimate shadow between Solley's thighs. Gin swallowed hard. Her captivation puzzled her. So did the increasing awkwardness she felt around Solley. Normally she wasn't the type to encroach on another's personal space, but she found herself drawn to Solley, eager for a smile or a word.

She'd seen sparks of the real woman buried under the crushing anxiety Solley seemed determined to carry alone, and she wanted to see more. She wanted to win this woman's trust and help her, but instead she had failed her somehow. Perhaps she was being overly sensitive because Solley seemed to be mad at her most of the time. She had a right to be upset about Jed and Will, but Gin sensed there was more to her prickly mood than the minor injuries her children had sustained and the fear of consequences from Dan.

Gin backed up a step, all too aware of spying on Solley as she puttered about in the kitchen baking cookies for her kids. Imagine if she were caught. How would she explain herself? *I'm like a moth. I know I could watch her this way forever…*

She was so engrossed, she didn't notice Janie helping a stiff and sore Marsha along the veranda until she met their mystified stares. They peered past her to see what culinary spectacle had caught her attention. A blissfully unaware Solley was still bent over the oven.

Gin gave a tight, polite smile and quickly walked away. Her escape wasn't fast enough. Janie and Marsha's voices carried as they trailed after her.

"Was Gin checking out my sister's ass?" Janie sounded shocked.

"Please," Marsha muttered, "even I check out your sister's ass."

❖

When the cookies were reduced to a plate of crumbs, Solley took her kids down to the shore for one last splash before bedtime. Standing there casually watching the loves of her life bounding through the breaking waves, laughing and shrieking at the antics of Nelson, Solley felt a great melancholy descend. So much was up in the air, she didn't know when she'd be able to bring the children back here again. Soon they would have to go home and face an uncertain future. The thought made her eyes sting, and she quickly blinked away her tears as she heard footsteps behind her.

She turned to find Gin standing silently, watching the kids frolic.

"Oh, I didn't realize you were there." Solley was surprised that Gin had joined her, after being snapped at in the afternoon and ignored throughout dinner.

"I won't interrupt." Gin's voice was warm. "I just wanted to apologize again. In your situation, I'd have been pretty angry, too."

Solley sighed heavily. "I owe you an apology. I'm just strung out these days, and foul tempered. I know it was an accident. If you're not used to being around children, they can lead you a merry dance."

A hauntingly sad smile passed across Gin's face and for a moment it seemed she was going to speak, but she shielded her eyes and looked out at the orange-hazed horizon. Watching her, Solley was perplexed. In profile, Gin's face seemed serene, yet Solley was certain she could detect a current of deep emotion just beneath the tranquil surface. She almost asked what was wrong, then bit back the question. Perhaps the answer was obvious. She'd made it pretty clear that she didn't trust Gin with her children and, at the same time, Gin genuinely seemed to like them. Most adults wouldn't even try to handle the Rayner brood, but Gin actually initiated play. And the kids loved her.

Solley pondered that fact and realized she was bothered by her children's instant adoration of Gin. They were wildly impressed with an adult they'd just met. They saw Gin as a hero, yet Solley was the one who weathered the daily challenges of motherhood. Their adulation had triggered something in her, an emotion that made her feel small and petty. Jealousy. With a stab of guilt, Solley saw that she'd blown today's events out of proportion to justify keeping her kids at a distance from Gin. How pathetic. Apparently she was more emotionally vulnerable than she'd thought.

Trying to backtrack a little, she adopted a conciliatory tone. "It's not your fault I'm a wreck, Gin. I feel like my whole life is balanced on a knife edge. Still, that's no excuse for behaving like a bitch to you."

Gin's expression changed as if she'd resolved something deep inside. Renewed energy literally pulsed from her and her whole face lightened. "I have an idea. What if maybe I gave you a trip round the bay in one of the power boats?"

It wasn't at all what Solley had expected her to say, but her dark eyes shone with excitement and promise and Solley was drawn to the idea. To the woman. But almost as soon as she recognized the fun, hope, and positivism of the suggestion, she heard herself squelch it. "No way, we'd lose everyone overboard."

"I meant just you and me." Gin refused to give up. "Things are sort of tense between us and I'd hate if we started avoiding each other. It might be nice for us to get a little space alone and maybe start again."

Was she talking about a date? Solley's throat clamped closed over a weird giggle.

Gin shuffled a little when there was no answer. "What I mean is, I really want to contribute to your family vacation, but now I feel like I'm detracting from it. I just want to do something nice for you. I know where some harbor seals sun themselves."

So, it wasn't a date, just a nice gesture. A reasonable, mature human being would say yes. Solley took a deep breath. "Thank you. I'd love to go look at the seals."

A blazing smile split Gin's face. "I'll catch you tomorrow afternoon, then?"

"Okay, it's a date." Solley's mouth dried as soon as the words spilled out. A date? "I mean, I'll see you tomorrow."

She didn't wait for a reply. Mumbling something about the children's bedtime, she strode off down the beach, disturbed by her own amazing emotional shifts. One minute she was mad at Gin, the next she was agreeing to a nature expedition. In all honesty, she didn't know what she felt and her confusion was worrisome. She needed to be making plans and getting her head clear so she could return home with some confidence in herself. She couldn't afford distractions, and that's exactly what Gin Ito was.

Solley stopped to retrieve pairs of discarded sandals and rinse them in the surf. Her kids gathered around and Nelson bounded up, all tail and wet coat. Everyone clustered close together, covering their faces as he shook himself free of sand and water.

Observing the small tableau from her vantage point, Gin felt her heart squeeze, as if in a vise, at the simple domesticity of Solley and her children. She felt curiously drawn to this young family in a way she didn't fully understand. Granted, she genuinely cared for them and ached for everything in their world to be all right. They deserved happiness. But she also had the bizarre sense that her fortunes were somehow tied to them.

Her gaze shifted to Solley. Her hair shone, haloed in the setting sun. Tall and tanned, she glowed with heat and passion. But sorrow and despair also weighed on her. Perhaps that explained the connection Gin felt. Supposedly misery loved company. She struggled to process her thoughts. Before she'd arrived at La Sirena Verde, she had spent several months in a state of bleak torpitude, unable to face work, people, life in general. Her depression had been so deep this time, all she could think about was the child whose warm body she no longer cradled. Her son, Miki.

Gin breathed the name, unwilling to lend her voice to it and hear the familiar sound float away. Like everything else of her son's, she held the name close and could not let go. Filled with grief, she returned her attention to the Rayners once more. She knew she was using them to salve her pain, but it was hard not to.

All the same, they were dangerously vulnerable and Solley didn't need anything else complicating her custody problems. If Gin really cared about them, she needed to leave Solley alone, not take her out on a boat so they could have private time away from the children, just the two of them. What was that about?

Forcing herself to turn away from the small family group, Gin walked into the darkness, mulling over the answer to that question. She wanted to be with Solley because she was attracted to her, and suddenly she wanted so many things back in her life. Love and laughter. Caring and commitment. In fact, she wanted a whole new life. And someone special to share it with.

Did these new urges mean her heart was finally healing? And if so, was she ready?

CHAPTER FIVE

Janie decided to take things into her own hands the next morning. No more beating round the bush. There was lustiness in the air, she could sense it, and she was going to get to the bottom of it. There was only one way to find out if her sister was truly abreast of the situation, and no more thinking in puns either. She poured coffee and waited for the aroma to lure Solley into the kitchen.

"So, what's going on between you and Ms. Small-Dark-and-Plummeting?" she demanded as soon as her sister showed her face. "Don't think I haven't noticed."

"What the hell are you talking about?" Solley glared at her.

"You've got the hots for her. I recognize that 'Chase Me, Charlie' look in your eyes."

"Rubbish. Where Gin Ito's concerned it's more like 'Kill Me, Charlie.'"

"You'd jump off that balcony yourself if you thought you'd land on her."

Solley groaned. "You are so off line about this."

"I am never off line about you, sister dear." Janie renewed her head-on assault. "I can read you like a book, and at the moment that book is a well thumbed copy of *The Joy of*

Lesbian Sex. You're harboring torrid thoughts for her, and if you want my opinion—"

"I don't," Solley cut in. "Trust me, I can see where you're going with this."

"Then admit it, you need to have a fling," Janie said briskly. "It's time to move on and have yourself a little fun. You've been miserable for way too long. Years, in fact."

"That may be so, but a quick screw on the eve of my divorce is not going to help me one little bit. Dan may not give a flying fuck, but I do. And please, no more of your love advice. It stinks."

"If anyone deserves a flying fuck, it's you. And believe me, if anyone can give you one, it's a stuntwoman," Janie threw back. "You haven't been serviced in years. If you were a car you'd be illegal."

"Well, excuse me." Solley sprang up. "I have neither the wish or need for a fuck. Flying, stationary, or otherwise. I'm here with my children for a family holiday of rest and recuperation, and that is *all* I need. That woman will be the death of us. Everything she touches turns to Neosporin." Solley scowled before coming up with yet another defense. "*And* I've heard of her reputation. The last thing I need is to be another notch on some super dyke's bedpost."

"That gossip about groupies and affairs with actresses is just industry spiel and tabloid crap. Marsha says she likes you, and I agree. So go for it, Solley." Janie leaned forward, softening her voice. "Two can play Dan's game. Let her see that. Have a fling and be happy."

"You're wrong, so drop it. I don't think about Gin that way," Solley lied. "I think of her more as a land mine."

Janie merely wiggled her eyebrows suggestively. "Explosive, eh?"

"Oh, wake up and smell the java," Solley huffed back. Aggravated, she stomped off, taking her coffee with her.

"Oh, wake up and smell your knickers." Her sister's parting shot scorched her ears.

❖

The lazy morning matured into a particularly hot afternoon and Solley slid into the veranda hammock, still bristling from her sister's insensitivity. Swaying gently in the breeze, observing the kids splashing in the surf with Nelson, she allowed the soft swing to soothe her frayed nerves. Gradually she drifted off to the lullaby of surf, gull song, and the happy voices of her children.

A flash of heat raced through her. It felt like a blaze of strong sunshine burning her up. She looked down past her marvelously flat belly to find its source. A dark head was buried between her thighs. A mouth sucked on her, the thick tongue occasionally breaking away to lap at her, encouraging her flow. And flow she did, sweet and moist. She was saturated. Hot and fluid. She was water.

Without warning, her mysterious lover's eyes opened and locked with hers. She found herself falling into the endless midnight of Gin's inky irises, drawn down into infinite darkness. Deep bliss. She was melting away in surrender…

Solley started awake with a befuddled orgasmic moan. Blurry and blissed out, she blinked directly into Gin's curious gaze. She froze, trying to focus. What just happened? What had she done?

"Are you okay?" Gin was sitting on the nearby deck chair with a newspaper and cool drink, one eye on the playing children. "You were moaning a lot. I changed the parasol angle in case you were overheating. It's a really warm day."

Totally flustered, Solley sat up. She knew her face was scarlet. "What time is it?"

"You've been sleeping for nearly an hour." Gin smiled

across at her. "Are you sure you're all right? You look a little spacey. Did you have a bad dream?" She sounded genuinely concerned.

Solley was speechless, jerked from the physical immediacy of her dream and rolling back down to earth on the soft breeze and the sound of Gin's voice. Her shorts were glued to her inner thighs. She needed to change her clothes.

"Still on for the boat trip?" Gin asked.

Solley searched her face but found no hidden intent; the question was innocent. Still dazed and disconcerted, she eased out of the hammock. "Yes. Do I have time for a quick shower?"

"Sure. The breeze is cooling now, so the wind on the water will be lovely. But bring a shirt, just in case."

"Okay." Solley brushed rapidly past Gin and practically ran from the deck.

What was wrong with her? It had to be hormones Yes, hormones. Even her dirtiest dreams could be explained in the light of her nonexistent sex life and reawakening libido. She cursed her sister's subliminal manipulation. With Janie rushing her toward a fling, she now felt embarrassed about the boat jaunt. And despite her physical urges, she was uncomfortable with the entire concept of sex with another woman. It seemed she still had a period of adjustment to go through. It was true that she had a tentative attraction to Gin, but that was as far as it went. Solley was content just to feel attraction for another woman again, any woman. For too long that part of her had been frozen. She'd given all her love and devotion to her children, slowly and systematically closing down the passion and desire her partner no longer wanted from her. It was strange; no, it was frankly terrifying, to feel that fluttering in her stomach when Gin smiled at her, to watch her hand gestures while she talked, and to be unable to look away from her graceful, athletic body when she moved.

So what, if Janie had a point? Solley couldn't see herself having a fling just for the short-lived satisfaction of sex and maybe a trace of revenge. Dan had written her off, but a lithe, hot stuntwoman like Gin could have anyone. If she was interested in Solley, what would Dan think of that? Solley immediately dismissed the idea. She wasn't in high school anymore. Trying to make Dan jealous was stupid. If Dan cared, she wouldn't have hooked up with her latest trashy bimbo, one in a long line of "lingerie models." If *lingerie* was French for "cheap tramp," that is. Younger, thinner, and stupider, Trixie had Solley beat on so many levels, but being bitter wasn't going to resolve the current dilemma. She didn't want to sleep with Gin just to prove something to Dan, or herself.

As she reached her bedroom, she resolved to put Gin to the back of her mind, treat her as a friend and nothing more, and concentrate on the kids. It was their vacation, after all. Later, when her world was safe and ordered again, she could pull her Gin fantasy out and examine it like a holiday photograph. Until then it would stay safely tucked away in her wallet.

❖

Gin was right, it was much cooler on the water. As they bounced across the bay, skimming over the topaz-etched waves to Seal Rock on the far western edge of La Sirena Verde, Solley even managed not to think about the kids more than once or twice. Truth be told, she was finally relaxing into the idea of letting them go off without her. Janie and Marsha had taken them to the cheesecake store in town. The worst thing that could happen was a stomachache.

The visit to the seals was great fun. The smelly beasts twisted and glided and played, in the hope of being fed. Solley was disappointed that she hadn't thought to bring anything for them to eat, but Gin said, "If they get lazy and expect food from every passing tourist craft, they'll come in too close and get cut by the propellers."

They spent over half an hour idling, watching the young pups play and talking about Gin's work.

"Did you always want a big family?" Gin asked, after they'd been silent for a while.

"I guess I did," Solley said. "It's great being one of three sisters, and I didn't want Jed to be an only child. I had him from a heterosexual relationship before I met Dan."

"So you two had the twins together?"

"Yes, we used a donor." Sensing an unasked question, Solley said, "Dan liked the idea of kids. The reality was less exciting."

"She's an idiot."

"Thank you, that's what I think, too. Unfortunately she's found another idiot. Younger, no kids, will never ruin her perfect body by having kids, but likes the idea of playing dollhouse with mine. So I'm about to start a very bitter custody battle. Dan wants the children fifty percent of the time, but she's planning to move to the other side of the country. If she gets her way, the kids will be out there for half the year. It's stupid, disruptive, and impractical, but what does she care?"

"What will you do?"

"Well, I'll probably relocate. I can't have the kids split across an entire country, it'd never work. I work in human resources, part-time at the moment, but I should be able to pick up another admin job easily enough."

"But your family and friends are here. How can she be so selfish to you and the kids? They need their family, too."

Surprised by Gin's vehemence, Solley said, "Yes, they do. It's not easy having same-sex parents. We have them in a liberal school, and we're not around bigoted people, but they don't live in a bubble. They need the validation they get from family and the people closest to them. Dan just doesn't see it. She wants her new life along with the best bits of the old one."

"Discarding the difficult stuff?" Gin mused softly.

With a dry little laugh, Solley said, "It must be nice to be able to shed her old skin and crawl away, like the snake she is."

"I can see why you're so careful about their safety." Easing away from Seal Rock, avoiding its lethargic inhabitants, Gin gradually opened the throttle until they were heading out to sea again.

"Well, I'm the birth mother, so she'll have to get down and dirty to persuade a court to grant shared custody. But she has a killer attorney. That's why I'm freaking out."

"Does Dan really know what she's asking for, wanting custody for half the time?"

"Oh, she has no idea, and neither does that airhead she's screwing. Della will have them both catatonic within two weeks. It's almost worth letting Dan have her, just to see it happen. That would teach the bitches a lesson."

Solley stole a sideways glance from behind her shades at the woman expertly maneuvering their power boat. Strong brown hands held the wheel. Sunlight molded the well-toned contours of shoulders and biceps. Gin's scarlet bikini, and the white shirt flapping casually in the breeze, displayed her muscled yet feminine body.

Solley guarded her appreciative gaze. She was enjoying their outing so much she didn't want to unsettle the comfortable rapport between them. Still, there was no reason she couldn't flex a little oomph muscle. *It's not like I'm tempting fuckicide or anything, just seeing if the ole girl's still got sex appeal left.*

She lounged back, the warm wind whipping through her hair. Gracefully, she extended her long tanned legs, her best asset, and curved her bikinied body into a sensual stretch, together with a pretend yawn.

The boat bounced hard over a large wave, and Solley's ass left the seat and came thumping back down with a decidedly unsexy whack.

"Sorry, didn't see that one coming." Gin glanced at her apologetically. "It caught you good, huh?"

Solley's skin pebbled under Gin's gaze rather than the cool seawater. Her caramel-colored swimsuit was now soaked a deep toffee. Beads of water quivered on her bronzed curves. Secretly she was pleased that her mishap had scored a warm flash of those dark eyes. Flirting mildly with Gin felt safe, and her confidence was slowly beginning to build.

"If we go out round the point into Cherry Cove we can tie up at the pontoon at Charlie's Bar and grab an early cocktail?" Gin said above the thrum of the motor.

"Yes, a cocktail sounds lovely."

They'd brought water to sip, but a late afternoon drink at the famous floating bar seemed a decadent and fantastic end to their relaxing afternoon. Okay, so it wasn't a date. But this little sliver of quality time definitely had her looking at Gin with new eyes. Fresh eyes, even. *And* she'd flexed a tiny bit of flirtin' muscle. She remembered her new mantra and applauded herself inwardly for at last being a little braver.

❖

"Is it bad to be having so much fun without my kids?" Solley's fingers slid slightly on the moisture-beaded highball glass as she sipped her daiquiri.

Gin laughed. "Everyone needs a break, even you. You're on vacation, too, don't forget."

Smiling, Solley shifted her gaze from Gin's distracting body to the floating wooden starfish that was Charlie's Bar. A long walkway connected the popular venue to the shore, so the sun seekers of Cherry Cove could dawdle up for a colorful beverage when they needed a break from sand and surf. The cove was a loud and busy public beach, a complete contrast to the quiet and solitude of the privately owned La Sirena Verde. Well, quiet when a stunt crew wasn't filming there.

Small craft bobbed alongside, allowing the crew to step along the pontoons to the central circular cocktail bar. The gentle Pacific roll that made Cherry Cove so popular among swimmers also provided the bar's occupants with a soothing sway. Lounging under the cool shade of the thatched parasol roof while being caressed by warm breezes, made Charlie's one of the most pleasant places to stop by for a drink.

"Thank you for the afternoon," Solley said. "It's been great fun. I loved seeing the seals up close."

"When I visit here, I always go out to watch them. I could sit for hours just listening to the gulls and the waves against the hull. Next time we should bring the kids." Gin broke off, realizing there might not be a next time. Embarrassed, she fiddled with her straw, not sure how to rescue the conversation. "Sorry, I was just thinking, if there's some time in the future when we're all visiting again…"

Solley let her flounder in silence for a few seconds before taking pity and rescuing her. "Hey, let's not invent more troubles than we already have. This is an afternoon for my memory book, a lovely day to look back on, no matter what happens. So, thank you."

Relieved, Gin grinned. "Janie said you'd love it."

"Janie?"

"Yeah, she suggested it. She thought it would do you good to get away from the kids for a while."

Anger swelled like a flood tide in Solley's chest. Janie had set her up. That interfering, matchmaking little sneak. Why couldn't she just let her make her own decisions in her own goddamn time? Hiding her irritation, she smiled sedately at Gin before downing her drink in several long, angry gulps.

Gin blinked at the decimation of the cocktail in seconds flat. "Can I get you another one?"

"No, thank you. It's getting late and the kids are bound to be home by now. Maybe we should get back."

"Oh…no problem." Gin looked a little confused. "Is everything okay? Did I say something?"

"No, not at all."

Solley wished Gin hadn't picked up on her souring mood. It piqued her that Janie wasn't far wrong about her frustration level. Hadn't she just preened in the boat for Gin like some witless bimbo, all legs and tits? It was pointless to deny that she was sexually attracted to the woman. And if Janie had seen how deep it ran, who else had noticed? Solley felt dismayed and exposed…and horny. Incredibly, hopelessly horny. Damn it!

CHAPTER SIX

The last rays of the sun had just dipped below the horizon when Solley and Gin finally strolled up from the jetty toward the house. The evening air was warm, and the sound of happy voices and the smell of barbeque drifted over the dunes to greet them. It felt good, like truly coming home.

Simultaneously, they smiled at each other, eyes locking for the merest instant. But in Solley's guts that brief glance felt like a year-long fall down a dark well. She put the children to bed soon after dinner, and Marsha and Janie retired early, too. Gin went into town with a few of the crew members for a drink and work gossip, so Solley found herself alone. She sat outdoors, contentedly listening to the waves, finishing a beer. Sometime after eleven o'clock the pad of quiet footsteps on the deck behind her announced Gin's return.

"Hey, there. Everyone gone to bed?"

"Yeah." Solley's pulse surged off the meter. Trying to sound casual, she said, "Want a beer? There's plenty in the fridge."

Gin went into the house and returned with a beer for each of them. She sat down beside Solley on the top step. "It's a beautiful night."

"It is. I'm so lucky Janie and Marsha have a home here. And that they like being invaded by visitors."

"Me, too. Your family has made my summer." Gin smiled shyly. "And I've really enjoyed getting to know you."

Their eyes locked and Solley felt the reverberation of her dream, deep inside her belly. Her breathing became shallow as she gazed into the same black depths that had monopolized her afternoon. Reason and logic drained away with the suction of quicksand. Time, and the world around her, seemed to freeze. Mesmerized, she was drawn irresistibly toward those eyes and the warm, full lips just inches from her own. Gin's dark gaze encompassed hers, silent and unwavering.

This is how she does it. Solley's last coherent thought drifted through her head as she slowly leant forward, her eyes locked on the beer-moistened lips. *She hypnotizes women into being sex slaves.* This was what fuckicide felt like.

As their lips softly touched, Gin gave a small involuntary gasp, and Solley, driven by years of lackluster love, deepened the kiss passionately. As she slid her tongue across Gin's lower lip, she heard a muffled sigh and Gin grasped her shoulders, gripping her tightly. Her urgent response and deep moan were rocket fuel to Solley's ardor, and she intensified the kiss. Her red-hot temperament not only emerged in anger, it was also the source of a dormant but volcanic passion she now instinctively unleashed. A dam had burst. Never had she felt so blissfully out of control. This was pure, unadulterated lust.

White light seemed to streak through her fevered mind as she fumbled with the tiny buttons of Gin's fine cotton shirt. After a sharp tug, the garment parted to reveal small, firm breasts topped with deliciously dark nipples. Solley's hurried attentions hardened them, extending the taut tips. God, Solley groaned, how many years of worship had made them so firm and long? They were like cigar butts. Pulling one into her mouth, she bathed it with hard strokes of her tongue as she rolled the other between her fingers.

She heard Gin mutter her name between soft cries. The hands kneading her shoulders trembled. Abandoning the succulent breast tissue, Solley ran her tongue from clavicle to earlobe. Gin groaned again and Solley became aware of frantic hands pulling at her, squeezing her upper arms. Words cut into her consciousness.

"Solley, we can't do this." Gin's voice was thick and throaty. Her skin was flushed and heated, her dark eyes glowing and unfocused.

"Why?" Solley drew back, breathing hard.

"You've made it clear what the risks would be. I want to make love with you, but I know what's going to happen tomorrow. You'll wake up in a panic and tell me your life is ruined and you're going to lose your kids because we couldn't keep our pants zipped up."

Aghast, and sick with desire, Solley objected, "No, I won't."

"Please. You lost it over a Band-Aid on Jed's wrist."

Solley scrambled upright, adjusting her disheveled clothing, her face hot. She wanted a meteor to fly out of the heavens and hit her right now. Or she wanted to crawl into the sand dunes and curl up and die. She couldn't bear to look at Gin's half-naked body. *Half-naked 'cos I stripped her. I ripped her shirt. There are probably buttons on the other side of the bay. And I nearly sucked her tit off.*

Solley didn't know what to say. Gin was right. She overreacted to every little thing concerning the kids. And her fears had cost her what she wanted most, to feel like herself again, a desirable, interesting adult woman. She'd spent so long being a mother she'd almost forgotten how it felt to be Solley Rayner. Radiating a humiliation she thought could probably be seen from space, she felt like crying.

Gin straightened her shirt. "I understand that breaking up

is rough and you need comfort and reassurance. I can offer that as a friend, but I'm not willing to have sex with you, then be discarded because you got what you needed. Or is this some kind of experiment? You want to find out if you can be with someone other than your partner?"

"No." Solley threw up her hands. "It's not like that at all. Can't we just admit we're attracted and do something about it?"

"If I slept with every woman who hit on me, I'd have to live in bed."

Solley vented her misery in angry sarcasm. "From what I've heard, I'm surprised I've seen you upright."

"So, now this conversation is about me being a slut?"

"Believe me, it's not only conversation."

Gin stood up. "You're the one who jumped on me, Solley. And if I'd been willing, would this have been a risqué holiday fling for you?"

"Risqué? This is my life, you idiot. If I'd thought, for even one second, that you weren't *willing*, I wouldn't have touched you with a gator pole, never mind—"

"Tearing my shirt off?" Gin raised her eyebrows. "And for the record, I'm not unwilling. But one of us has to act responsibly."

Waves of shame flooded Solley again. "You're right," she said stiffly. "I don't know what I was thinking. It won't happen again." *'Cos I'll have died from shame by the morning.*

An uneasy silence descended, broken only by the muted crashing of waves on the shore. Standing very still, Gin gazed at the skyline, her stomach churning. She wasn't sure which of her emotions was more powerful. Desire? Resentment? Jealousy? It bothered her intensely that she had to walk away from a world of possibility because of Solley's ex-partner.

Filled with mixed emotions, she glanced down at the woman who'd ended her neutral detachment from the world..

Solley sat huddled into herself. She wore so much hurt, Gin felt angry. It was clear that Solley desperately wanted to find happiness and for her family to stay together, and that she'd lost most of her confidence. *I'd love to be your hero but I'm too fractured, too weak.*

"You're beautiful, and I wish we'd met under different circumstances," Gin said quietly. "Dan's a fool, losing you."

The awkward silence sneaked back as Solley digested these last shy words. "Thanks…I think."

"I mean it. I'd walk a mile in Dan's shoes, given half the chance. But it's not my gamble to take. I know that with you the kids always come first, Solley, and I respect you so much for that."

Solley hesitated. Wanting Gin to see her and the kids as separate beings, she steered the conversation away from her role as a mother. "Well, despite all the lumps and bumps, and breaks and…blindness, the kids seem to think you're the best thing ever. Seriously, this may end up being one of their last summers here, but thanks to you, they'll always remember it happily. You've salvaged summer."

Her expression was so full of genuine warmth and affection, Gin almost reached out for her. "No, I think you've salvaged me," she said honestly.

Solley seemed troubled as she gazed up at her. She started to speak, but fell silent. With a small, sad smile Gin wrapped her shirt more closely around her, murmured good-bye, and headed off into the night.

Dismayed, Solley stared out at the inky sea for a while, then trudged indoors. She turned off all the lights and checked the locks before dragging herself dejectedly upstairs. Passing her sister's bedroom, she heard the muted thud of a headboard against the wall. Muffled moans accompanied the rhythm. Brilliant, even the physically incapacitated were having sex. Weren't couples in long-term relationships supposed to lose interest?

Seeing Marsha and Janie so content, and obviously still hot for each other, normally made Solley happy. But tonight all she could feel was a dull envy and a rising anger that she and Dan had allowed their sexual relationship to slip away, just like everything else that had tied them together. Everything except the kids, and it was wrong for children to be little more than ballast weighing their unhappy parents down enough that they stayed together. Would she rather settle for that than make a clean break?

She moved heavily toward the bathroom in a miserable mood. She'd been brave, she'd taken the big plunge, and she'd landed splat on her stupid face.

Looking dispassionately at that same stupid, freckled face in the bathroom mirror Solley felt like the ugliest, most inept person in the world. She couldn't take any more risks. There would be no bumping into Gin, accidentally or intentionally. No stealing long looks at her enigmatic, soul-destroying androgyny. Her coal black eyes. Her small, beautiful breasts with those large rock-hard nipples that fit so perfectly in Solley's mouth. There would be no more addictive kisses.

She groaned out loud, torturing herself with salacious thoughts that only made her wetter, and hornier, and even more frustrated. Would she ever be able to look at a Havana cigar again and not cream her jeans?

❖

Filming halted the next day by midafternoon, as the light began to fade rapidly and a cold front blew in across the bay, promising thunderstorms later.

Gin sat side by side with Marsha on the cliff top location as the crew rushed around, packing up before the bad weather arrived. Leaning back on her elbows, she asked, "Tell me how you and Janie met."

"You were there when we started dating."

"Yeah, but I didn't pay attention until you were a couple, sort of solid and complete, like you'd been with each other for ever. Know what I mean?"

"Yeah." A soft grin covered Marsha's face. "You know, sometimes I have to think really hard about life before Janie. It's like I was just standing around wasting time, waiting for her. I didn't know I wasn't happy. Didn't know what love was. I didn't even know I was waiting. And then one day she just arrived and there was no way I was ever going to let her go. I'm not so stupid I can't recognize love."

Gin gazed out toward the bruised horizon, watching the storm clouds roll in. "Has it been all you hoped?"

"And more. Some mornings I wake up so light and happy I think my heart will pop. I look out the window and bless all my days since finding her. Some nights I fall into her so deep I'm scared I'll lose myself and never find my way back." She paused, loosening the laces on her boots. Today was the first day she'd been able to wear them since the accident. "She expanded my emotional vocabulary."

Gin met her steady gaze with wonder. Marsha wasn't the sentimental type, but she seemed to be reaching for the words to explain her feelings. "I understand. At least I think I do."

"I know." Marsha chuckled. "Pretty weird, huh? I never ever thought I'd be talking like this one day. I didn't think I could feel so much, so deeply. But I'm so much in love it scares me, even after all these years. And it's not that I think she might leave me, because she never would. We've barely begun to scratch the surface. It's growing every day."

Marsha tilted her head back, allowing the cool breeze to ruffle her long, dark curls. "So, other than my relationship history, what's on your mind?"

"Solley Rayner."

"Hah!" Marsha's expanded emotional vocabulary bit the dust. "I knew you two were getting it on."

Gin shook her head. "No, we're not getting anything on. She'd like to, but it's just sex to her. A fling to ease her through a tough patch."

"And that's a problem because…?"

"Aren't the complications obvious?" Gin couldn't explain that somehow Solley had jump-started her heart. That she'd delivered a kick up the ass that made her terribly aware of her stunted life and frozen emotions. "The partner is a problem."

"That's history." Marsha gave a dismissive snort. "Dan was never cut out for family life, anyway. Solley's the one who holds it all together."

"Because her children come first. That's another issue," Gin said seriously. "I look at them and I'm filled with laughter and joy, no tightness, no pain, no guilt. I'm light. And when I'm with her, and with them, I'm happy. I can't explain it, but everything is vibrant and new." Mystified at the clarity of emotion in her own words, she said, "I want it to stay that way. I don't want to mess things up."

"Things are already messed up. Sleeping with her isn't going to change the situation or ruin your connection with the kids."

Gin shook her head. "You know that's bullshit. Sex changes everything."

Marsha shrugged. "Then I guess you just have to ask

yourself what kind of risks you're willing to take. It's funny, I've never seen you back off like this when you want something."

"Maybe if all I cared about was a quick fling, this would be easy. But you know what you were saying about falling into someone and losing yourself? I guess I'm afraid I'd…fall into her. In fact, I know I would. I can feel myself going there already. And what if I did, and then it all went bad? I really don't think I could handle that, not on top of losing Miki."

Marsha studied the surf far below them. "Gin, I know there's no time limit on grief, after a loss like that, but it's been four years. I haven't seen you this animated, or interested in anyone, since it happened. That means something, don't you think?"

They sat on in silence until Gin felt she could continue. "We quarreled."

"Sounds like a good start."

"Her relationship isn't the only problem. You know what it's like in our business. The gossip." Gin rolled her eyes.

"It's not like you give them anything. But that's the problem with don't-ask-don't-tell, they make up whatever stories they want. If you don't have a man on your arm they assume you have a woman on every finger."

"They can say what they like about me, but Solley has kids."

Gin could imagine the gossip if they were seen together looking like more than friends. She wasn't out, publicly, but her closest friends knew she was a lesbian. She knew a lot of gay people, supported LGBT causes, and had a big gay fan base. The tabloids loved to drop hints about her "close friendship" with any female star who spoke to her. It was ironic. She was virtually celibate, taking time to herself while she tried to restore her emotional balance.

"Solley's been hiding behind those kids for too long,"

Marsha huffed. "For crying out loud, don't you start using them as an excuse, too. You have to take a chance, Gin." She stated the no-frills obvious with an honest heart. "You can't keep living like this. It's time."

Gin shifted uneasily beneath her speculative blue gaze. "But it's not the right time for Solley. She can't take a chance. At least, she can't take a chance on me."

CHAPTER SEVEN

K elly Rose arrived at the trailer camp two days later in a black stretch limo, with an entourage of press and studio reps.

"This is the side of Marsha's business I just can't stomach," Janie sermonized. "That someone gets paid such an obscene amount of money for looking good and acting stupid. At least Marsha truly earns every bruised and bloodied cent they pay her."

She had already said she wasn't going to hang around for the schmoozing once the presentation was over. She didn't lower herself to such "bullshit" and was going to head into town for a protest shop at her favorite boutiques.

Solley had no such compunctions. She wanted to drool over her favorite overpaid, good-looking, stupid-acting screen idol up close. It also seemed appropriate to be present, since Gin was going to receive an award.

"What's it for, exactly?" she asked Janie as they gravitated toward the makeshift stage, along with crew members and fans who'd heard the star was coming by.

"It's the Indie Pendant Film Award for best stunt director. Gin's won it for *Russian Rebels*. Since she can't make it to the award ceremony, Kelly Rose is presenting it now and they're filming the thank-you speech for the show. I hope it cheers her up some. She's been moping like a rain cloud for days."

"Great."

Solley was pleased about the award, but ecstatic that Gin's frame of mind was as gloomy as her own.

She'd often watched the awards event live on TV. It felt strange to think that to the rest of the world, not just her children, Gin Ito was an impressive person. In getting to know her—if ripping off someone's shirt and sticking her tongue in their mouth was *knowing*—Solley had forgotten she was pretty goddamn famous.

In front of rolling cameras and a barrage of flashing press photographers, Kelly Rose sashayed up to the stage. A skintight sundress advertised all her charms, as well as the skills of her cosmetic surgeon. Batting impossibly long eyelashes, she posed for her audience, swamping them all in a smile as bleached as her hair. She was, Solley decided, living proof that the cloning crossover between human DNA and Barbie doll plastic was indeed possible.

An elbow nudged her ribs. "Guess who's going to meet your favorite heroine?"

"My heroine?" A series of flashbacks and fantasies flew through Solley's mind. Gin plunging into the sea from a helicopter. Gin diving into the water from a moving speedboat. Gin abseiling freeform down a cliff face. Gin's lithe, naked body spread out across the sand dunes. The two of them, kissing…

"Kelly Rose, dufus." Marsha squinted at Solley as though trying to make sense of her distracted response. "She wants to talk to the stunt crew personally. The team works on most of Kelly's films, and she likes to keep things sweet. It's just a PR exercise, but I thought you and the kids might get a kick out of meeting her."

Solley brightened. The day was getting better and better. First, Gin was miserable, and Solley didn't care if her kitten had been run over, as long as she felt like crap, too. Second, Solley's favorite actress was here and maybe she would meet her. She watched Kelly Rose present Gin with a trophy shaped like a silver pendant flag. She wasn't close enough to hear the speeches the smiling pair made to the cameras, but she was uncomfortably aware of the body language between them. Kelly Rose clung to Gin's arm like Glad Wrap, the side swell of her impressive bosom crushed against Gin's tight bicep. She flashed a humongous amount of dental porcelain in Gin's face.

Yes, they were just a little bit too close for comfort. Their physical messaging spoke louder than words, the decent words found in a dictionary, that was. Watching them gaze at each other like meerkats in heat, Solley closed her fists. Her temper sparked, fueled by the gasoline vapor of jealousy. She knew she was glaring with narrowed eyes and that her feelings were probably obvious to all around her, but she couldn't hide behind a smile.

As the crowd began to drift off, she fell in with them automatically. Any desire to move forward with Marsha and the kids to meet that floozy hanging off Gin's arm had completely disappeared. Plus, the temptation to thrash Gin with a camera cable was too strong to keep in check. Deep in murderous thought, she found she'd fallen in behind a couple of familiar-looking young women, the two she'd overheard bitching about Gin the previous week. Sure enough, parts of their gossipy conversation floated back to her.

"They've been an item for years, right back to *Princess of the Pacific.* Gin did all the pearl-diving stunts for her, if you know what I mean." One sniggered to the other.

Oh, my God, don't they have anything better to do? It's

disgraceful. Solley maneuvered herself closer so she could hear better.

"Well, I heard she does more than her fair share of sucking up to Ito."

"You mean she likes to eat o' Ito."

They both giggled over the terrible pun.

"You need to suck up real good if you want Gin to dive for you. She's not cheap."

"I'd let Gin dive on me anytime. Hell, she could plunge on me from that helicopter of hers."

Oh, for God's sake, she couldn't plunge your kitchen sink.

"It must be a hard life when you've got Kelly Rose constantly kissing your ass."

"Maybe not a hard life, but a hard *something.*" More sniggers.

"Did you see Kelly rubbing her tits all over her arm back there?"

"Talk about marking your territory. Why not just pee on her?"

Solley had heard enough to make her mood even darker. *I knew it. That horny, fake bitch is panting after Gin. Not that I give a rat's ass.*

She swung away through the dunes, her huffy steps kicking up sand. She didn't see the woman lying belly-down in the dune grass until she nearly fell over her.

"Hey, watch it!" the stranger objected. "What's with the sand-kicking? I've got valuable equipment here, not to mention my eyesight."

"Sorry, I didn't see you. Talk about camouflage." Solley took in the lean young woman sprawled in the sand. Sawn-off surfer-dude pants and an Army tank top showed off a tanned, muscular physique. Her mid-brown, blunt-cut hair framed a cute face complete with baby dimples and expressive gray eyes. She had an expensive-looking camera and telephoto lens pressed against her shoulder like a weapon.

"Why don't you just stick a big fat marker in the sand so everyone knows where I'm at?" the attractive stranger complained. "Get down, woman."

Well, I never thought I'd hear those words this week. Solley complied, feeling rather silly to be prone in the sand next to someone she'd never met. "I take it you didn't get a general press invitation?"

"Oh, the invitations I get usually involve the use of forceps just to extract my camera."

"Paparazzi?"

The young woman offered her hand. "They call me Sniper, but you can call me anytime," she said with easy confidence.

Solley shook hands with her. "Solley Rayner, and maybe I'll just call you fresh. So, Sniper, why are we crawling around out here in the sand?"

"Right now I can only think of one good reason and at least forty positions." Sniper's gray eyes twinkled mischievously.

Solley decided to ignore the outrageous flirting. "What I mean is, half the world is going to see the presentation tomorrow night on TV. Hardly groundbreaking news, is it?"

"Ah, that orchestrated love fest down there doesn't interest me. I've got bigger and better prey in my sights." Sniper gently tapped the lens.

"Like what?"

"That would be telling. And who exactly would I be telling it to, Ms. Solley Rayner? What's your role in *Red Revenge 2*?"

"None at all. I'm just a gawping bystander. I'm vacationing here. Thought I'd drop by to see the illustrious Kelly Rose in the flesh."

"Well, watch the daily papers this week and you might see just that. I'm targeting that trailer there." She indicated Gin's trailer. "A little birdie told me Ms. Rose will be 'in the flesh' sometime soon, along with her intense little body double. No one's caught them in the act, so far, but I intend to hit the headlines. This will be so hot off the press the paper will combust."

"And how did you come by this hot tip?"

"Let's just say I have a reliable source." She shrugged casually. "Besides, everyone in the biz knows what's going on behind closed doors. It's hard to prove, but maybe this time I'll score, so to speak." She turned her smoky gray eyes on Solley, and a thoroughly charming grin lit up her face.

Seems everybody's scoring this week, except me. Solley smiled ruefully at the young woman and her suggestive eyes. "Well, I'll wait with bated breath for the press release. I'd better be getting along."

"Hey, maybe we'll see each other again."

"If we do, you're obviously doing something wrong, G.I Joe," Solley flung over her shoulder. She crawled away on hands and knees, unwittingly giving Sniper a delectable view of her swaying rear.

"Seriously, where are you staying? Maybe we could meet up for drinks…or something?"

Solley delivered a barefaced lie. "I don't drink."

"Well, what about the 'something'?"

Solley just laughed. "I don't think so. See ya, Sniper."

There was no way she going to play with this dangerous young charmer. She was horny, not stupid.

❖

Later that afternoon Solley sat on the veranda swing with her second spiced rum and Coke, replaying the conversations from earlier in the day. Something didn't add up. Gin's big spiel was that she was protecting, not rejecting Solley, but the whole world seemed to think she and Ms. Silicone Valley were an item. Why couldn't Gin just say she already had a lover?

Solley snorted to herself and realized she was getting tipsy. That was fine, she needed to unwind. Looking out across the sands, she was surprised to spy Gin striding in her direction, a big smile on her face, her arms filled with packages. The warm breeze lifted her hair as it gleamed in the sun, moving it fluidly, like liquid ink. The pale blue cotton shirt fluttered over her white tank top, displaying tantalizing glimpses of muscular shoulders and chest. Sea green bikini shorts hugged her hips and enhanced the well-toned sweep of her tanned thighs.

A hot little sigh escaped Solley as the object of her lust and dejection drew closer. She took another sip of her rum and Coke and thought of the never-ending gossip about Gin's amours and her supposed liaison with Kelly Rose. Paparazzi always had their finger on the pulse. Well, that Sniper would have her finger on everything she could. Solley pictured her on her belly, half buried in the sand like a sexy little sphinx.

Solley gave a sharp gasp as she added two and two. Gin was obviously hiding her secret affair with Kelly Rose behind a smokescreen. She'd lied about everything, including her reasons for not sleeping with Solley, no doubt to protect the "star" from being outed. Anyone earning as much money as Kelly Rose did whatever it took to maintain the right image.

Solley could understand Gin's desire to keep their privacy intact. She just wished Gin had trusted her enough to tell her the truth, or simply to say no without an explanation. Why invent the elaborate fiction about pretending to care but wanting to protect her and the kids. Jeez, it wasn't like Solley couldn't take a bruising. Even if Gin wasn't seeing Kelly Rose, obviously the last thing she would want was a tired old leftover like Solley hitting on her.

See what happens when you try to be brave? her demons whispered.

Solley's new mantra shriveled up. She felt foolish and humiliated for kidding herself.

Meanwhile, a happy and confident Gin mounted the veranda steps, arms full of bodyboards and kites she'd ordered for the kids. It was really their mother she'd come a-wooing, and the way to a mother's heart was always through her children. The smile on her lips faded as she met Solley's stormy glare head-on.

"Is something wrong?" She faltered. "Has something happened to one of the kids again?"

"Have you seen the kids recently?"

"No, not since this morning." Gin felt stress mount in her body.

"Then they're probably all right." Solley dripped sarcasm.

"Sol, what's wrong? Where are they?"

"They're still at the camp with Marsha. Stop pretending you give a damn. Why aren't you there…with your girlfriend?"

"Sorry?"

"Oh, I assure you, you will be." Solley bit back a reference to Sniper's planned exposé. She flung herself onto her wobbly feet and stomped off to refill her glass.

Confused, and concerned by Solley's slightly unsteady gait, Gin deposited her packages and followed her to the kitchen. "How many of those have you had?" she asked as Solley mixed a generous rum and Coke.

"Enough to make me finally wise up to you. Think I don't know your little game? Well, I'm not stupid. Everyone else knows, too. Ha!"

"What are you talking about? What's got you so mad?"

"I think most of today got me mad. I met a photographer.

A cute, sexy woman who's interested in me." She slapped her chest. "And she gave me the lowdown on you and Ms. Slutty Rose, not that it's news. Half of Trash Town down there," she waved vaguely toward the movie camp, "was bitching about it."

"Who are you talking about?"

"Sniper, with the beautiful smoky eyes."

"Sniper?" Gin was immediately alert. "Keep away from her, Solley. She's dangerous. She wants insider information on the movie and she'll use you to get it."

"She can use me any which way she wants." Solley took another big gulp of her drink. She was buzzing. It was definitely time to slow down. "I'm not gonna be pushed around and lied to anymore. Not by Dan, and definitely not by you."

Solley's accusations ricocheted around Gin's head as she grappled with the angry words. "Sniper's shooting in the dark. Look, I don't know what she's told you, but you can't trust a word she says. There's nothing going on between Kelly and me."

"What a hypocrite. I can't trust *her*?" Solley waved a finger in reprimand. "In fact, I'm going down to the dunes right now to find her. And maybe get some sand burns." She swerved toward the door.

"Solley, no." Gin grabbed her upper arm, holding her in a firm grasp that hinted at the strength underlying the smaller woman's physique.

Solley tried to struggle free but realized she was going nowhere while her arm was clasped in Gin's grip. "Why'd you lie?" She turned her anger on her captor. "It's not like I'm afraid of rejection, you know. For years I've watched my partner's desire for me atrophy. After I had the twins my body disgusted her. She never touched me or wanted me the same way again." Anger ran away with her. "So I understand lack of desire. I understand loss of love and respect. I understand being second best. I understand losing, period. What I don't understand is why you bothered to lie to me when all you needed to say was 'I don't want you.' Why the phony care and consideration? I don't need your fucking charity."

"Solley…" Gin was stricken.

"Oh, forget it. Fuck off back to your trailer. To your starlet. You can bend all your camp whores over backward, as far as I'm concerned. I'm not crying over *you*. You're really not that important. All I wanted was a fuck from the mighty Gin Ito. What's wrong with that? There seems to be a wait list. All I did was join it."

Gin's hand fell, allowing Solley to shake loose. Shocked by her own outburst, Solley stumbled toward the door, no longer sure where she was headed. What was wrong with her? Where did that come from? She didn't need to broadcast how she felt about herself, or her body, or Dan's opinion of it. She could take being turned away. She lived with it every freakin' day.

Before she could make it out the door, a pair of firm hands on her shoulders spun her round. Angry eyes locked with hers, swallowing her in their inky, infinite depths. Solley burned with fury, glaring right back. Her chest tightened, her heart pumping pure anger. But there was something else in the air between them, a current, an energy that crackled like the final moments of a burned down fuse.

Then Gin exploded. "You're the liar! I have no starlets. No whores. I'm alone. My child is dead. And no one will allow me respect or privacy to grieve. Because I have no male lover, I must be gay, so clowns like Kelly want to start a media circus about invented relationships. I can't find space to heal. I don't know how to heal. And then I meet you, you stupid, fucked-up madwoman. You and your crazy children."

"Gin, stop." Solley's feeble protest sounded like air hissing from a tire.

But Gin was unstoppable. Eyes gleaming like a demon's, she roared, "You're so wrapped up in your quick fuck, and your quick fix, and your instant gratification…so go on. Go find Sniper and let her shove her sandy fingers in you. I hope it soothes your ego, if nothing else."

Solley slapped her before she even realized her hand had moved. She stared aghast at the mark staining Gin's cheek. She barely had time to register her shame before strong hands grasped her upper arms and she was pushed against the pantry door. A calendar and several small leaflets shook from their pins and scattered across the floor tiles. Solley's protests died as Gin angrily claimed her, crushing her lips until she whimpered.

Gin drew back, still holding Solley's arms. She pushed her thigh hard against Solley's crotch. Their foreheads pressed together, eyes inches apart. Slowly she covered Solley's lips with her own, this time sucking, softly caressing, drawing out a delicious moan. She let her hands roam down to cradle the luscious rounded hips, pulling Solley closer.

Everything was a hot, horny haze to Solley. How had she ended up here, pinned against this wall? What the hell had she said to unleash this succubus from her fantasies into the real world? Her mind buzzed while her body burned. Her traitorous hands buried themselves in Gin's thick black hair, and she was guiding that searing mouth to the secret places on her neck that would melt her into total, slutty surrender.

"Take me to bed." Gin breathed into one of those warm pulse points before delivering a soft nip. "Now."

CHAPTER EIGHT

Gin's command was a sobering splash of cold water to Solley's overheated mind. She drew a sharp breath as a hot tongue traced her sensitive collarbone. Her skin tingled and her spine turned liquid.

"No." Only one feeble word struggled out of her locked throat.

Gin's lips hesitated in their nuzzling dance. "No?" she queried darkly.

"No, this is madness." Solley tried to disentangle herself, hands shaking. "You can't do this to me. Just three nights ago you pushed me away. You were being responsible. The big protector."

Gin tightened her hold on Solley's waist, keeping her pinned between her body and the door. "Three nights ago you ripped the shirt off my back. You were the one wanting this. You've just accused me of having numerous lesbian affairs, of not wanting you, of spurning you." She nipped Solley's full lower lip before soothing it with the tip of her tongue. "Well, I'm here and I'm yours. This is where I want to be. This will be whatever we make it."

Deepening the kiss, she poured herself into its melting sweetness, for this was the one that truly mattered, the seducer's kiss that would make Solley hers. She stroked a slow upward path from Solley's hipbone to the outer curve of a full breast. Cupping its weight, she gently moved her thumb across the raspberry tip. Her moan of pleasure merged with Solley's.

All Solley's resolve seemed to melt into her panties. She was helpless. Pliable. Lost and so, so hopelessly turned on.

They stumbled upstairs to Gin's room like trysting teenagers. Doors slammed and clothes were torn off and scattered as teeth and tongues swooped on every newly exposed inch of skin. They fell on the bed, twisting and turning, holding each other tightly, heads empty, hands and mouths full. The last vestiges of clothing pooled on the floor, and finally, with heated flesh, they brushed against each other.

A rush ripped through Solley's body and she pulled Gin into her arms. "God, you're so beautiful. I can't believe how much I want you. How you make me feel. It's been so long since I felt like this."

Gin gasped as the air was hugged out of her lungs. Growling playfully, Solley pushed her back onto the bed and crawled over her, eyes glittering with raw, primitive energy. Swooping with a hungry mouth, she drew in Gin's bottom lip, sucking on it thoroughly. Her hands pushed Gin's damp thighs as far apart as possible, giving her total access to the thick silken triangle and the juicy softness beyond.

Gin moaned deeply as molten lava scorched through her veins. She felt herself grow swollen and wet under the bold gaze burning over her sex. Desire coursed through her. Every nerve snapped and sang. Gin's heart lay swollen in her chest, bursting with emotion, the desire was so raw in her. And she was acting on it, breaking out of her comatose life and reaching out unashamedly for what she wanted. Braving the future, daring it to make her regret this moment. This was her first step into a new life. She was amazed to be taking it, hand in hand with Solley.

Leaning back on her knees, Solley let her eyes feast on the exposed flesh before her. She massaged the strong thighs with trembling hands. Gin's nipples hardened, stealing Solley's focus. "Oh." she groaned. "Oh, God."

These breasts, these nipples would always be her weakness, her total downfall, where Gin's body was concerned. If she never was allowed to touch this body again, this vision was what she would always carry with her, scorching her synapses every time she thought of Gin.

Beneath her, Gin undulated like water, soft and silken, pulsating with the rhythm of the persistent mouth tugging on her nipple. Her hands buried themselves in the curtain of flaming hair that draped silkily across Solley's shoulders. She drew Solley up begging for another kiss. She was so addicted to those opium lips.

Solley carefully reached down to pinch the moistened clitoris between thumb and forefinger, gently rolling it, causing Gin to jolt at such a direct touch. They locked eyes, and placing her hand to the dead center of Gin's chest, Solley held her down.

Stroking the engorged organ, she murmured, "I want you so bad. You make me feel so hot for you I can't believe it. And I want you to want me like that, too. I want you to think of me all day tomorrow. I want your body to hum whenever you remember what I'm going to do to you."

Gin's throat worked tightly as she swallowed. She wanted to speak, but she couldn't. With a soft groan, she touched the hand that covered her heart, sliding her fingers between Solley's.

"Relax, baby," Solley whispered. "Let me look after you. I want this to be good for you."

She pressed a long, sex-soaked finger against Gin's center and slowly, persistently entered her. Guided by the rhythm of Gin's rocking hips, she gently introduced a second finger after several strokes, spanning to touch the tight inner walls and fill her.

Gin gasped and squirmed. Her face was flushed, her eyes hooded with raw need. She shivered as the questing fingers found the spongy spot and began to stroke. Solley applied more movement and pressure. She let her free hand drift from beneath Gin's to cover one tempting breast. The nipple pushed up into the heart of her palm, and with a deep groan, she nuzzled the delicious flesh spread out before her.

Gin clung to her, pressing and circling her back and shoulders, holding her closer. As Solley slowly increased the pump, Gin uttered a small cry and one hand flew back, gripping the bedpost until her knuckles shone white.

Solley remained magnetically drawn to the stiff nipples, squeezing and flicking each into jutting arousal. "I just can't leave these babies alone. I swear, if I could put them in my pocket, I'd take them with me."

Gin's head swam. Her skin felt so burnt she swore it would crawl off her body and curl up under the bed. The air seemed to be solidifying in her lungs, her chest heaving to suck in each breath and then force it out. Solley's fingers continued their full plunge while her tongue ravished Gin's breasts with long sweeps. Then cool air spun across her chest as Solley shifted downward. Her hot breath caressed Gin's sex. The tongue that had thrashed her nipples now lavished long firm strokes over her engorged clitoris. White light shone behind her eyes. Her juices slickly lubricated Solley's fingers as their rhythm increased inside her. The suction on her clit was practically unbearable as it was pumped by possessive lips. Her hips rolling uncontrollably, she bucked up into Solley's mouth, belly rippling with effort. Drying saliva kept her nipples puckered rigid.

"Solley. Oh, Sol. Oh…" Her litany rang around the room.

More white light, then flashes, colored flashes, beautiful… "I'm coming, I'm coming. Oh, God."

Her entire body spasmed, contorting on the bedspread into a deep, soul-ripping orgasm. She gripped Solley's hair, keeping her mouth glued to her. Shuddering, she let out a long moan as a languid tongue was drawn one last, nerve-shattering time along her twitching sex.

The power, the taste, the scent. Solley reveled in this woman. Triumphantly, her lips and chin slick with Gin's juices, she crawled up her body, grinning like a lunatic. Gin pulled her into a deep kiss, licking her own taste from the curved cheek and bowed lips, sucking her saltiness off Solley's tongue. She wanted more. She wanted to gorge on Solley's moist scent, to bathe her face between those long, tanned legs and nestle between the smooth thighs. With easy strength, she slid down so that Solley straddled her shoulders. The wet folds she coveted pressed against her eager mouth. Gin took her time, slowly exploring as Solley rocked gently back and forth.

Gripping the bedrail, Solley felt Gin's tongue deep within her, circling and flickering and pushing her higher. Firm hands on her butt cheeks held her in place, fingers biting deep into her flesh, allowing her just the minimum of movement while her pelvis screamed to thrust and plunge. Instead she was impaled and exquisitely tortured on this pliant spike of succulent muscle. Head flung back, she moaned at the ceiling. All the years of nothingness rolled away, the aridity of her love life, her uncertainty in her sexual being, a loneliness so deep she thought nothing could ever touch it. Like rainwater filling dried-out riverbeds, swirling into hollows and crevices, seeping down into cracked earth saturating dormant roots, a tide of renewal pounded through her. Hot, thick blood replenished every chamber of her heart. And, as her sense of self brimmed over, so did her eyes, until huge fat tears slid down her face.

Gin's hold relaxed and she moved her mouth a fraction to suck Solley's thoroughly swollen clit. A long, low groan rose up through Solley and almost immediately turned into a strangled cry as she wailed out a guttural orgasm. Her thighs quivered and her breasts mashed against the cold iron of the headboard as she arched and shuddered in absolute release.

She had wanted to last a little longer, to savor the wonderful tenderness of the woman nestled between her thighs. But her emotional needs were too raw, too close to the surface. Raised like scars, pebbled like Braille, they crept across her skin, leaving her open and interpreted to the loving brush of Gin's fingertips. Exhausted, she fell into the arms waiting to hold her and hid her tearstained face in Gin's soft neck. Her heart raced wildly until she could finally breathe control back into her body and accept the sated happiness that cocooned her.

❖

Much, much later, with her head on Gin's shoulder, Solley casually played postcoitus with the small taut breasts and their dark stubs.

"I was so jealous first time I touched these. I thought about how many lovers had squeezed and sucked them. And seen how long and sexy and…chewable they are. I wanted to be the only one to know those things. Now, after sex with you, I just want to light 'em up and smoke 'em."

Gin laughed, her breasts quivering. "They're never usually like this unless I'm aroused. I was mortified that night when you pulled my shirt open and there they were, aiming straight for your mouth. I knew then I was in big, big trouble. It seems my tits have all the brain cells."

"Girl, if you only knew my lurid plans for you that night. I was going to devour you, cannibalize you, keep these for my pleasure alone." She idly tugged a nipple. "Make them mine, all mine."

"Oh, damn." Gin suddenly remembered she had a calendar, a job, and an existence outside of this bed. "Speaking of possessiveness, I was supposed to meet Kelly half an hour ago."

"You must be devastated." Solley smiled. Sniper wouldn't be happy, either, to lose out on her front-page scoop.

"Well, it's too late now." Gin gave an unrepentant shrug. "I'll call and apologize later. I'm not even sure why she wanted to see me."

"Maybe she didn't paw you enough this morning."

Gin grimaced. "She seems determined to fan the rumors about our supposed lesbian affair. To be honest, I don't trust her. She's a real media slut."

She relaxed in Solley's arms once more, and they lay in silence watching the early evening shadows creep across the wall.

"Tell me about your child," Solley asked after a while. "Did you have a boy or a girl?"

"A boy, Miki. He was born with a congenital heart defect. They tried surgery, so he spent a lot of time in pain, in the hospital. He died just before his second birthday."

The words came out flat and even. Her face was calm and composed, but Solley knew currents of deep pain ran underneath the still surface, turbulent and sucking. Clutching at the living. Dragging the sufferer down into dark, airless depths. Solley couldn't imagine coping with such a loss. She was scared to imagine it, to place herself in Gin's shoes and picture one of her children gone.

"I'm so sorry, Gin."

"Thank you." Gin's eyes seemed to swallow all the shadows in the room. "He was gorgeous, and so brave. He had the most wonderful smile." She broke off abruptly. "See what happens? Sometimes it feels like yesterday, but it's been almost four years. I should be coping better. But it floods back like a big black wave, crushing me, squashing all the air and light out of my life, and I get scared I'll never surface again."

"Isn't that natural?" Solley said carefully. "You're still in a grieving process."

"I don't know. Every time I start to feel as though I'm finally getting through it, I seem to end up in another deep depression. There's no pattern to it, no trigger that I can see, except for his birthday and the day he died. This summer began like that. I just fell into a black hole. Knowing I was going to be working here at La Sirena Verde was the only thing that got me through."

Solley hesitated. Should she ask? But she was burning to know. "How do you feel now?"

"Right now?" Gin smiled broadly. "Lighter. Happier. Looking forward to tomorrow. Meeting you and the kids sort of lifted me out of that hole. It's hard to be in a funk when they're around. And this." She tightened her arm around Solley. "This, today was…perfect." Her words slipped away into an intimate silence. She wanted to say more but needed time to process the roller coaster she'd been on since the moment they'd met.

"Who was his father?" Solley hoped she didn't sound too inquisitive.

"Someone who helped me when I decided I wanted a child, no strings attached. We're not in touch."

Solley was familiar with the situation. She and Dan had conceived the twins that way, and Janie and Marsha now had the same plan.

"I'm a very private person," Gin said. "Hardly anyone I work with even knows about Miki, apart from Marsha."

"She and Janie never said a word to me." Solley respected

the strong bond between the three women and was in awe of the painful secret they'd all carried.

"That's why I trust them. Marsha got me through. It's amazing, I know she hides behind this big, dumb, softy front, but when the chips are down she is *there*." Urgency entered Gin's voice, as if she had to get the whole story out. "He was so ill, I just walked away from everything so I could spend every minute with him. That's why there are rumors, I suppose."

Solley felt incredibly out of touch. All it had taken was three kids, and eight years as a mom, and she'd lost her grip on popular culture. She wondered which rumors Gin was talking about. Maybe Kelly Rose wasn't the only actress she was involved with, according to the media.

Gin must have sensed her uncertainty. With a wry grimace, she said, "I mysteriously disappeared, then returned without explanation, and I wasn't in rehab. There's bound to be speculation."

"But you're not an actress. It seems bizarre that you can't have a private life."

"The media follows me because they think I'm the key to outing an actress. There's enough gossip about my sexuality to make stories like that sell."

Solley thought of the two silly women she'd overheard. They didn't know Gin but had drawn the obvious conclusions. Frowning, she recognized that after hearing them for the first time, she'd seen Gin differently. Not just as a generous, friendly woman, but a sexual being.

"I fell for the idle chatter myself," she confessed. "I thought you were the sexiest lesbian on the planet. I couldn't believe you had any interest in me. In fact, I still can't."

Gin's hand found hers. "You're beautiful to me, Solley. Inside and out. Don't ever doubt that, or forget…*this*."

Perfectly sated, they lay quietly in a calm, luxuriant

afterglow until Solley asked in a small voice, "Saturday night…why did you stop me?"

Gin paused, calling upon her courage. "Because, despite all the rumors, as I said…I don't sleep around. I didn't want to be a summer distraction."

She swallowed a procession of silent pleas, alarmed by a reckless impulse to let them spill out. *Please don't let me be a distraction. Please let me be real to you, because I'm falling for you, and I need you, and because I can't believe this could happen so quickly.*

Maybe her powerful attraction to Solley was a trick of the heart to quiet the desperate, ugly neediness inside her. Or maybe she simply needed to feel something, anything, after years of numbness. Whatever the basis of her feelings, Gin was shaken by the certainty that she would turn her world around to have Solley in it. But her world was an empty place, and Solley's was full of people she loved and who loved her. Although her life was a struggle, she was trying not to let it all fall apart through her divorce. And at least she lived it, in all its pain and pleasure.

"Oh, Gin, you *drive* me to distraction. Don't you know I'm now your alpha groupie? You make me feel so goddamn good, and that's official." Solley gave her a big hug, and Gin's heart fell twice: first in love, then into another abyss.

CHAPTER NINE

E arly the next morning, Solley and Janie took their coffee out to the deck to sit and watch Gin bodyboarding with the kids in the surf.

"Ah, this is what vacationing is all about." Solley leaned back, contentedly watching her hot, secret lover splashing about in red bikini trunks and a tight navy blue T-shirt. *Hey, look at me. I've got a hot, secret lover!* She was glad her sunglasses hid the lust she knew was burning in her eyes.

"You're in good form today." As usual, Janie's snoop-o-meter had picked up on the emotional vibe. Her intuition was an uncanny gift, but one she never used in the fight against evil. Rather, it was employed for gossip, rumor, innuendo, and Janie's vicarious thrill-seeking through the sexploits of others.

"I slept well," Solley said. It helped that she'd had hot sex all afternoon and most of the night with her new lover, but she wasn't going to share that salient fact with her sister.

"Uh-huh." Janie eyed her suspiciously, the super-senses on alert. She knew something was up, and given a little time she'd get her answers. Solley was just too easy to play. With an innocent air, she remarked, "Kelly Rose is looking for Gin."

"She's here?"

Janie gave a vague, uninterested nod. "Marsha says Sniper was floating around on the dunes yesterday. She's a paparazzi, a real stalker."

"What do you think she wants?" Solley tried to sound nonchalant.

"What do you think?" Janie rolled her eyes. "She's trying to catch Gin and that tramp with her pants down. If Kelly has any say in the matter, she won't have to wait long."

"Are you saying Kelly *wants* to be outed?"

"Who knows what goes on in the mind of a publicity junkie with the IQ of a gnat? Sniper may as well be her private photographer."

Solley glanced toward the dunes. If Kelly was hanging around, Sniper probably wasn't far away. "Well, if they think they're going to get her in a sleazy pose with Gin, they're kidding themselves." She got to her feet. "Where did you say Kelly was?"

"She could be down at the jetty." Janie poured herself another cup of coffee. As Solley started walking, she called after her, "When I said she wants to be outed, I didn't mean she hopes just *anyone* will jump her."

In a flashback to their adolescence, Solley flipped her sister the bird and casually exited the deck. She circled the dunes without seeing Sniper, then headed down to the old jetty. At a glance, the place seemed deserted, but then a figure moved into view and Solley found herself alone with the blond and beautiful Kelly Rose. Wrapped in a silk shawl, Kelly gazed moodily out to the horizon as though stood up by a movie hero.

Ah, this must be The Rendezvous That Will Never Happen, Solley thought smugly. *Or perhaps* The Trap That Will Never Snare, *or* The Tramp Who Will Never Be a Lady. Y*ou won't be able to set Gin up for your paparazzi buddy today.*

"It's beautiful, isn't it?" She couldn't help but speak up

for the beauty of the place, and for some reason she couldn't quite fathom, she wanted this tramp to register her presence.

Kelly immediately swung around, but her welcoming smile stiffened and disappeared when she didn't recognize Solley. "Are you supposed to be here? This is private property, you know. Not open to the public."

Annoyed, Solley moved further onto the jetty until she faced the haughty star. "As a matter of fact, I do know. My sister owns this part of Topaz Bay."

Something registered in Kelly's icy blue eyes, which immediately sparkled with malice. "Ah, your sister's the one who sleeps with Marsha Bren?"

"Actually, she's Marsha's partner, not her concubine," Solley retorted, her dislike for this woman going all the way down to her taproot.

"Honey, in this business they're all concubines." Kelly smirked coolly, starting to turn away with a show of boredom. "Rich or poor, they're all alike, all whoring for a piece of Hollywood ass."

"Well, you can vouch for that better than me. I mean, what with you having your nose up against it all the time." Solley smiled sweetly. *Don't you badmouth my sister, you studio whore.*

"Why, you ignorant nobody," Kelly spat, not fooled by the clumsy innuendo for one moment. "I should get security to remove you."

"What's security gonna do, throw me off my sister's property?"

Even as Solley retorted, Kelly tried to swoosh indignantly away, but the narrow jetty inhibited her angry movements. Spitefully, she elbowed Solley in the midsection, trying to lever more room as she passed.

Swearing inwardly at the sharp dig in the ribs, Solley responded with the slightest, itty-bitty bump of her hip. But with her being a big-boned, bad-tempered gal, even the tiniest nudge managed to totally unbalance the strident star. Kelly Rose tottered for one frozen moment, then windmilled frantically before spinning off the edge of the jetty in a graceful arc of silk and squeals.

Solley knew the water was warm and barely waist deep. Even so, she momentarily considered hauling the actress out of her predicament and apologizing. After a nanosecond of soul-searching, she decided karmic justice had prevailed and spun on her heel, leaving the howling actress splashing and cursing behind her.

As she strolled away, she yelled, "Welcome to the Rayners, bitch!"

❖

By midmorning, Gin and Marsha had been summoned back to the movie camp. It seemed Kelly Rose had departed abruptly, bumping the schedule forward by a few hours. Still twitching with guilt at dunking a minor celebrity, and struggling to hide an overabundance of pent-up sexual energy, Solley went for a short stroll to the rise overlooking the expanse of Topaz Bay. She needed time alone to go over every detailed minute of the past twenty-four hours.

She had barely taken in the spectacular view, when she heard her name hissed from one of the nearby dunes. Grinning, she mounted the crest to meet the impish gaze of Kelly Rose's pet paparazzi.

"Hey, Sniper. You're way too easy to find. You need some twigs in your hair and boot polish on your face."

"I don't need the combat gunk, thank you. I got skill, sweetie." She grinned cheekily, her eyes roaming Solley's curves.

"Too much skill, from what I've heard." Solley wondered how much she could learn if she could make this woman lower her guard, not that she doubted Gin's word about Kelly Rose. But after Dan, it was hard to trust anyone completely. A part of her seemed to crave extra reassurance. In a light, teasing tone, she said, "I've been warned to keep away from you. It seems you take no prisoners."

"Oh, it's the total opposite. I've been told I'm very captivating."

"I have no problem believing that. I bet you're honeyed flypaper."

Sniper shrugged. "I'd rather be a Venus flytrap. One step outta place and…snap." She swung her camera around, aimed it at Solley, and shot off a series of pics in quick succession.

"Hey, quit that."

"They're for my personal catalog. Keeps me warm on cold winter nights." Sniper grinned. "Don't suppose you'd contemplate taking your top off?" She raised her eyebrows hopefully.

"Do you want a slap?" Solley was not as annoyed as she pretended. She wasn't used to overt sexual attention and found it more flattering than perhaps she should.

"Okay, Sparky." Sniper flung her hands up in a conciliatory gesture. "Look, come here. Let me show you something." Returning to her belly, she waved Solley over to join her.

"Here." The camera landed in Solley's hands as she stretched out beside the photographer. "Look out there, across the bay." Sniper leveled Solley's head and adjusted her angle. The telephoto lens zoomed in on the waves in amazing detail.

"Wow, this lens is powerful. What am I meant to be looking at?"

"To the left a little." Sniper's body pressed full length along her back. The brown head rested beside hers. Sniper's breath brushed past her ear as a smooth, tanned hand directed the camera. "See, a little ways out...dolphins."

"Oh, yes, I see them." Solley felt Sniper's weight push gently down onto her buttocks. Then a very slow, undulating grind into her behind. She lowered the camera and growled, "Sniper, get off my ass or I'll shove this lens where your flash don't shine."

"What the hell is going on here?" Janie's indignant voice boomed from directly behind them.

They both jumped guiltily. Sniper flew off Solley's prone body, grabbing for her precious camera.

"Brilliant. While you're up here with your dirty little peep show, your daughter has just drifted out to sea on a bodyboard," Janie barked out.

"What?" Solley leapt to her feet, clawing her way out of the sand dune, photography and flirtation instantly forgotten.

"Hey, wait up." Janie jogged after her. "Don't freak. Marsha and Gin were there. Gin swam out and she's bringing her in right now."

Solley was only slightly placated. "Can't I leave my damned kids with her for five minutes without something going wrong? That's every one of them she's managed to jinx. She'll be accidentally burning down your AI clinic next. What happened this time?"

"Della thought she saw sharks and raised an absolute hullabaloo. There was never any danger. Well, except she may have broken her drama bone."

"What do you mean? Is she hurt?"

"You'll see soon enough. I knew you couldn't have gotten far, so I came after you." She managed to sound sarcastic even through her puffing. "Luckily, I heard your voices in the dunes. I didn't know you were into photographic modeling."

"Oh, shut up." Solley could hear her daughter's yells and squawks before they could even see the surf.

Rounding the last clump of dune grass, Solley registered the small melodrama before her. Marsha and the boys stood on the beach along with several onlookers. Out to sea about two hundred meters, Gin was skillfully redirecting a bodyboard back to shore. Astride it sat a semihysterical Della. Nelson dementedly dashed in and out of the surf, barking until Gin had maneuvered close enough for him to swim out and add to the chaos.

Finally Marsha paddled into the shallows to secure the bodyboard as Gin got to her feet with the wailing child in her arms. With Della clinging to her like a little monkey, she waded ashore and headed directly for Solley.

"What on earth?" Solley reached for her daughter.

"Gin saved me, Mommy." Tears ran down her little face, breaking Solley's heart. "There were sharks…" Hiccupping started and her words were lost.

"Those weren't sharks, honey. They were dolphins. And they would never hurt you. And Gin got there first."

"H…how do you know they weren't sharks?"

Solley chose not to reveal her up-close and personal dolphin photo shoot. "I've seen them on the Discovery Channel. They were definitely dolphins."

"It was a discovery, all right," Janie muttered from a few feet away.

Gin glanced up at the comment. Solley threw Janie a hard look and she backed down. Nobody needed this right now.

"Let's get her into the house and calmed down," Gin said.

Looking around, Solley knew she was right. As long as there was an audience, Della's dramatics would continue until she was truly hysterical. She needed peace and quiet.

Allowing Gin to carry Della to the house, Solley took her hand, and the rest of the family trailed after them. Covertly, she lifted her eyes to scan the dunes above. Somewhere up there, Sniper Jones lay secreted. Solley could only hope this domestic melodrama would be of no interest to the celebrity stalker.

❖

Lunch was served on the deck. Della sat cuddling Nelson in the veranda swing, spoilt at being the latest victim of the Rayners' vacation of doom. Solley sidled up to Gin where she sat perched on the railings sipping a beer, looking peaceably out at the azure horizon.

"Thanks for hauling her back in. I take it she wasn't in any mortal peril, despite the stage school audition."

Gin grinned, shifting over to allow Solley to sit beside her. "Stage school would be worth considering. She's got more than her share of dramatic flair."

Solley smiled back, watching the sunlight glint off Gin's dark, sexy eyes. She let herself revel in a rush of pure undiluted lust, when another more subtle emotion welled up. Tenderness. She felt tenderness for the woman who had protected her child when she wasn't there. Who had reached out for her, at one of the loneliest, most lost times in her life. Gin was so kind and sweet, Solley really, really liked her. In fact she trusted her with the people she loved most in all the world. How was that possible after such a short time? Had having great sex already demolished her common sense?

"What's wrong?" Gin asked. "You're looking at me strangely."

"Nothing, just some silly thoughts." Solley cleared her head and her throat. "What are you doing later, hot stuff?" She lowered her voice, lust rushing back like spring tide. "Want to sneak off to a sand dune tonight?"

Gin discreetly cupped the buttock perched on the railing next to her. "Just come to my room?"

Solley hesitated, "No. Someone might see." She threw a quick glance at her sister and her partner.

"So? What's the problem?"

"There isn't one. I just want this to be our private business."

"But it's only Janie and Marsha—"

"No. Please. I just want it to be us, okay?"

Gin looked confused and upset. Solley wanted to reach out to her, to touch her face and look into those hurt eyes. To take her words back. But she had her reasons.

"Please," she repeated. "You of all people should understand. I just want to keep this to myself…until I get used to it."

Gin nodded. "I understand. Your secret's safe. But my room is secluded at the other end of the house. If you need me, that's where I'll be." Though her posture was relaxed, her eyes sparked with challenge.

With a wink, Solley moved away, swaying her hips for Gin as tantalizingly as decorum would allow.

As she watched, Gin pushed down the burning fear rising in her chest. Solley wanted a dirty little secret. Nothing open, nothing honest. An affair conducted in the dark, with no light, no joy, to let it grow. The burning dropped to her gut and turned stone cold.

❖

Gin came through from the bathroom, naked after a quick shower, beads of water snaking down her dark skin. She hesitated. Solley stood in her room, leaning against the door, desire burning in her eyes. Gin approached slowly and lifted a hand to cup her face. They kissed softly. As the kiss deepened, they drifted onto the bed.

Gin started tenderly undressing her. Peeling off the T-shirt, she caressed and thoroughly licked the generous, lace-cupped breasts, pleasuring them until Solley squirmed. Gin unclasped the bra and eagerly gathered the creamy flesh that spilled out onto her palms. She dived on a candy-tipped nipple, pulling on it hungrily before moving to the other.

Solley moaned under the sweet torture. Her panties were discarded next, her legs lifted and spread over Gin's shoulders. A thick tongue broke through her folds and burrowed deep inside. She rocked on it as firm fingers rolled her nipples and massaged her breasts. She lifted her hips seeking out the teasing tongue, demanding more and more. A ripple of savage heat rolled through her as she studied the midnight head buried between her thighs. Overwhelmed by raw need, she opened herself wider, offering all. Arching her back and wringing the sheets with balled fists, she begged Gin to fuck her.

Three fingers were thrust in deep, taking her breath away. They were immediately clenched and swallowed up. Tipping her head, Gin sucked down hard on her clitoris, teeth gently encircling its base as she swirled and flicked her tongue. Solley's dance took her higher and higher, every nerve and muscle stretched and singing, until her orgasm ripped through her with all the intensity of an express train, seen from miles away but there in minutes, fierce, fast, streaking through her. Exploding her in ecstasy.

It took several seconds before she could even speak. "Oh my God. I've never come like that before. I thought I was dying."

Gin crawled up to lie beside her, grinning proudly at her ability to rock her lover's world.

"I don't know what you're looking so smug about," Solley warned with panting bravado. "When this arrhythmia stops I'm gonna fuck you till your eyes cross."

"Try me," Gin whispered in her flushed ear.

Without warning she was flipped over onto her back.

A grinning and remarkably recovered Solley hovered above her. "I think I will," she growled. "Roll over."

Gin trembled on all fours. She felt Solley's breath on her back. A small trickle of saliva pooled near her spine. A hot, wet mouth swooped to lick it away and bite her sweat-slicked flesh. Solley's fingers entered her from behind. Gin felt so exposed, so vulnerable. But longer thighs covered hers, rolling and rocking with her, forcing her rhythm, controlling her motion, blanketing her with care and desire. Two long fingers plunged in and out, in and out, their wet sucking audible above her low moans.

Her skin pebbled as Solley breathed words along her spine, making her tingle at the silken promises. That there would be more, always more. How she'd fuck her with fingers, and tongue, and toys. And stretch her slowly to fit her and her alone. Because Gin belonged to her. Whispering dirty words that thrilled with their taboo. God, how could Gin survive more of this sweet aching, sweet longing, sweet togetherness? Solley was in her blood like a virus, making her feverish, addicted, sick to the heart.

The first wave of orgasm rolled up from the depths of her belly and crashed through her like a thick, oily wave. With her head hung low and her body arched with pleasure, she convulsed on those long fingers that never ceased to play her. Crying like an animal, she shuddered and clenched, holding them in her as long as possible. Wave after wave rode over her until, at last, she collapsed, totally spent.

"I'm never going to get enough of you," she panted, wrapping her arms around her lover as she felt Solley's hand slip free of her. "That was fantastic. You're fantastic. We're fantastic. Sex with you is so fantastic."

As Solley stroked her sweat-saturated hair, Gin sighed contentedly and pulled her big bundle of flaming love closer, cradling her tenderly. They snuggled up in the after-bliss, content and sated. And yet Gin was troubled. She'd greeted Solley's appearance in her room with relief, unsure if Solley's wishes for their affair to remain clandestine would limit their time together. And though Gin wanted no limits, she understood Solley's hesitancy, her fear to commit at this stage in her life. How could she alleviate Solley's worries and show she would be there for her?

She scoured her mind for a way to share her thoughts. "You know how we've only known each other about two weeks—"

"Two weeks. Is that all?"

"And you know how the kids accepted me in no time at all." Gin was rambling a little now.

"Mmm." Solley cuddled in further.

"Solley, I believe in karma." Gin tried again. "It's a cultural thing. It brings the people and circumstances I need into my life, so my spirit can evolve and I can live well and help others. I know you've got to go back and deal with unpleasant things, with Dan and all—" She stopped as Solley touched her cheek.

"Don't talk about that, baby," Solley murmured softly. "It's awful out there in the real world and I don't want to go back. I want to stay here at La Sirena Verde where nothing is real and it's all just a beautiful fairytale." Her words drifted off.

Gin frowned, this was harder than she expected. "Fairytale? Like being rescued and living happily ever after in a magic kingdom sort of stuff?"

Solley mumbled something, but she'd slipped back into her cozy cocoon.

"Sol, I really do care for you, and I know it's a confusing time for you and the kids. I can't offer you a fairytale, but maybe I can give you some security, at least. And who knows, perhaps we'll find a happy ending after all this custody mess?" This was difficult, but Gin soldiered on. "Marsha and I want to open a stunt academy. That means I'll have to be around more, maybe even rent here in the bay for the rest of the summer. You and the kids could—"

A gentle snore alerted her that she'd lost her audience. Solley had drifted off to sleep midramble. Gin sighed. Her growing love for this crazy woman sprouted more tendrils at every opportunity, binding her closer and closer. Deep down, however, she had the nagging feeling that what she wanted to offer was not what Solley needed right now. Her fear of losing her children had frozen her. Gin could see she was afraid to move in any direction in case Dan pounced. She was scared of every scratch the kids acquired. Scared of saying or doing something wrong. Scared to take a lover.

Gin felt bitter, and deeply angry with Dan for doing that to her partner. For using Solley's love for her family as a weapon in an ugly divorce. And for trying to cheat her of her home, her children, her future.

CHAPTER TEN

M ommy?" Della asked, "Why are you wearing Gin's PJs?"

Solley froze in the act of sleepily pouring her morning coffee. Her face flamed. Janie's eagle eyes narrowed as she took in the blush and the midthigh silk kimono that would have been knee-length on its real owner.

Gin shuffled clownishly from one foot to the other. "I lost it in the wash," she blurted.

"I must have grabbed it out of the dryer without looking," Solley gushed immediately, despite the improbability of this claim. The damn thing was a heavily embroidered eggshell blue and not the sort of garment to be mistaken for the cotton shifts she usually favored. She had only just poured a cup of coffee, and already the day was going to hell.

There'd been no time to shower before she and Gin had to leap out of bed, scrabbling for clothes and alibis when they heard Janie yelling from the kitchen. Solley made sure to keep her distance from her sister, avoiding the customary hug. She didn't normally exude the smell of sweat and sex first thing in the morning, and Janie had already wrinkled her nose with a puzzled air a couple of times.

"Where's Marsha?" Gin attempted a masterful change of topic.

"She went down to Main Street to pick up her prescription. I swear, she's getting addicted to those painkillers," Janie griped. "I'm going to replace the next batch with placebo breath mints and see if she even notices."

"That seems kind of harsh if she's still in pain." Solley hadn't realized Marsha was being so stoic, playing with the kids and trying to get back to work.

Janie rolled her eyes. "It'll help her adjust. Besides, she gets all horny when she's pain free, and while I'm not complaining, I do need my beauty sleep. She can go all night if she gets the dose just right."

Solley spluttered into her coffee mug at this revelation. "Must we? It's kind of early for your 'I married a sex addict' confessions."

Solley and Gin swapped a conspiratorial look of relief at their narrow escape. Gin let her gaze sweep over Solley's body, lingering on the curves draped in the soft blue silk embroidered with dragons. They were barely out of bed and, already, Gin wanted her again. She could hardly believe she had only known this woman for a couple of weeks, the connection felt so deep, so instant. It had been wonderful holding Solley asleep in her arms. She thought back to her impulsive, sex-addled offer. Part of her was relieved that Solley had slept through her ridiculous musings; part of her was anxious that she was alone with her passionate feelings. She wanted to reveal all and get a measure of what Solley thought and felt about her…and the future.

She frowned. What had she really been offering? The happy-ever-after? The house by the sea? Did she really think she could simply buy happiness for Solley? Money had never brought Gin any true peace. Only standing beside Solley did that.

Solley watched the troubled look flit across Gin's face. Was she worried they had nearly been caught out? Why? She was the one who had wanted to gamble and meet up in the goddamn house. Solley was annoyed at herself for falling asleep instead of returning to her own room. She would have had a firmer handle on the morning if she hadn't woken up to Gin's kisses. But being in Gin's arms was becoming addictive, and it was harder and harder for her to keep a distance between them. Janie bellowing up the stairs was a wake-up call, all right. Solley realized she was crazy having an affair on the eve of her divorce. She didn't need this distraction. Okay, so maybe her body did, but reality was looming fast. Soon she would be back home and all this would be just the fairytale she'd drifted to sleep dreaming of last night. *Get a grip, Rayner. This vacation is about your kids, not about you and your never-ending neediness.*

She looked over at Gin, hoping to find something that grounded her, that pulled her out of her anxiety and fear. But Gin was frowning out the window, distant, detached, focused on the kids, who were trying to fly kites out in front of the veranda. As if sensing Solley's stare, she looked round.

"I'll go change and help the children with those kites," she offered. She had to get out of this kitchen and grab some fresh air. She felt she was suffocating in Solley's subterfuge.

"Try not to let anyone float away." Solley meant to sound like she was kidding, but there was an edge to her voice that made Gin stare at her for a few seconds too long.

"I think I can manage. I did okay rescuing Della yesterday."

"Gin, no offense, but every time you're in charge of my kids something vaguely catastrophic seems to happen. I mean, you might as well have gotten them a nuclear submarine as bodyboards. And sure, Della wasn't in any real danger. God knows, she can swim like a sewer rat. It was the shark thing that caused her to freak out. Even so, she was truly terrified and that's an experience I don't want my kids to suffer."

Solley knew she sounded ratty, but one of these days the minor accidents would become major and she would be sitting in the ER listening to Gin making excuses as if it was perfectly normal for children to hurt themselves every time they played. She had to remember she was the constant in her children's lives, their mother, the one who would always be there. Partners could come and go, and she would always be left to pick up the broken pieces.

"I love your kids. I protect them every way I can when they're with me." Genuine hurt gave Gin's words an edge.

"Oh, for God's sake," Solley snapped. "I'm merely asking you to be a little more aware, a little more responsible."

"I'll have you know I am fully responsible. My family is descended from samurai." Gin drew herself up to her full height, bristling with hurt and anger. This woman never listened to her when it came to the kids, no matter how important the things she had to say. "The Itos adhere to the samurai code of protection and social responsibility."

"More like the kamikaze code," Solley mumbled beneath her breath.

Gin stared at her in deflated shock. Where was this anger coming from? She wished she could keep up with Solley's mood changes. She'd been enjoying her new morning ritual of playing with the children before heading off to work. In her heart, she secretly hoped it might become a more permanent chore. But she still hadn't come to grips with how to avoid riling Solley. Marsha was always dropping hints about managing the quick-tempered Rayner women. Gin wasn't sure whether to start taking notes or accept the advice as a warning and back off while she could.

Before she could come up with a reply that would mollify Solley, Janie said, with the flippancy of a soon-to-be-parent who already knew everything, "God, Sol. You can't wrap them in cotton wool their whole lives."

"Excuse me, but you can save the parenting advice until you've had some practice with Junior M," Solley responded smartly, her maternal feathers ruffled. "Once your life and your sanity have been dismantled piece by piece, it'll be interesting to see who needs to be wrapped in cotton wool first, you or the baby. My money isn't on Junior."

She glanced around intending to say something softer to Gin, but she'd vanished. "Damn," Solley muttered. "Where did she go?"

"As far from you as she can get, I imagine." Janie raised her eyebrows. "You seem tense today."

"Guess we all are."

"Speak for yourself. I like to think I have that 'great sex' glow."

"Here we go again." Solley got up. "I need a shower." She flung past Marsha as she stomped out of the kitchen.

"What was that about?" Marsha dropped a bundle of newspapers, mail, and purchases on the counter.

"I have no idea, but I caught Sol in the sand dunes with a woman yesterday," Janie said. "I was going to tell you after I'd talked to her first. Guess that ain't gonna happen."

"No shit. Who was it? What were they up to?"

"Looked like a photographer, and they were grinding away back to front like humping ponies."

"Aw, fuck. It has to be Sniper Jones. She's such a little shit." Marsha groaned.

"Well, she better not screw around with my sister." Janie flared, recognizing the notorious paparazzi's name. "Solley's very vulnerable at the moment. I wanted her to have a little fun this vacation, to build up her self-esteem, but not with someone like Sniper. If she hurts my sister, I swear I'll bury her so deep in those dunes an archaeologist couldn't find her."

"Poor Gin." Marsha set about making fresh coffee.

"Why? What's it got to do with her?"

Marsha sighed. "I wasn't going to tell you this, but Gin's sweet on your sister. The whole family thing hit her hard in the heart."

Janie blew a long, low whistle. "Then it's a good thing Sol didn't take my advice and chase her."

"You told her to hit on Gin? Now? In her state of mind?"

"Why not? They both need to get laid. But Sol's so fucked up at the moment maybe it *would* be better if she fools around with a tramp like Sniper." She passed her coffee mug to her lover. "Oh, and I'll take that newspaper, too."

"Oh yeah? And does Madame want me to carry her out to the veranda and fan her with a palm frond while she reads?"

"Madame wants you to stop being a smartass and load the dishwasher…then come out and fan her with a palm frond." She took the *LA Times* from her partner and fished out the entertainment section. Spreading it flat on the table, she gasped, "Oh, my God."

❖

The entertainment section was to Gin and Marsha what *The Wall Street Journal* was to a stockbroker: all the idle gossip, deals, and news that could make or break the players, big and small alike. Janie was also addicted. Where else could you read the juicy details of a lurid celebrity divorce alongside the showstoppers and show-floppers? But the last sensational cheating spouse exposé was nothing compared to the headline that leapt from today's front page.

ALL NOT ROSY IN KELLY'S LOVE BED, the main banner screamed. A smaller headline underneath declared, "Mystery Woman Replaces Kelly Rose as Ito's Love Interest."

Janie stared in horror at a huge photo of Gin striding across the sand, a tearful Della perched on her hip. Solley was holding Gin's hand, and Will trailed behind them wearing the pirate's patch he refused to give up. Next to him marched a bandaged Jed. The photo was cropped to suggest an intimate family unit, a celebrity family no less, but a tightly unified one, pushing through a crowded beach toward sanctuary.

"Crap," breathed Marsha.

"There's more." Janie thumbed over the page.

There, etched against a beautiful sunset, was Solley, her hair shining in a luciferous halo. She grinned casually at an arm-flailing, mouth-gaping Kelly Rose, caught in a frozen fall off the old jetty into the waters of the bay. A companion pic showed a bedraggled, screeching Kelly standing waist-deep in water, her wet blouse clinging revealingly to her breasts, while Solley strolled straight toward the camera with a truly evil dominatrix grin. The sleazy layout looked like a poster advert for a lesbo porn site, and probably would be by tomorrow. The caption read, ALL'S FAIR IN SHOVE AND WAR!

"No wonder she left early." Marsha grabbed another newspaper from the stack and found the entertainment section.

This time the editor had run amok in Photoshop. A picture of Kelly and Gin hugging during the award presentation was cut away to a shot of Solley with her hands on her hips, glaring as though she was watching them in a jealous rage. Then came the "revenge" pic of Kelly's pirouette off the jetty.

"I don't believe this," Janie groaned. "She must have shot these from just outside our house. Now every crazy in the country will be camping down here." She nodded toward the movie trailers. "Like we need another invasion." She took a deep breath and turned another page. "Please God, let it be over."

Standing in the kitchen doorway, finger-combing her wet hair, Solley asked, "Let what be over?"

Janie and Marsha turned sharply around. Marsha placed both hands flat on the newspaper. At the same time, Janie tried to fold it closed. Their guilty faces spelled out the story before Solley even saw the headline. "Red*head* Revenge?" she read aloud.

"Someone's smart idea," Marsha scoffed. When Solley stared at her blankly, she added, "You know, we're filming *Red Revenge 2*, remember?"

But Solley had stopped listening. All she could see was her face, and her kids, splashed all over the papers. "What the hell?" She flew over to the table.

"You dunked Kelly Rose?" Janie gaped at her.

"She called you a concubine." Solley attempted to justify herself. "I just gave her a little bump with my hip. Her balance is shit."

She dragged the paper out from beneath Marsha's hands, mortified. She'd been caught red-handed "assaulting" the breasty icon of millions. And now she was being shamed in front of the entire nation.

"Who took all these?" she spluttered, hoping to move the blame and shame onto another.

"Your girlfriend, Sniper Jones, that's who." Marsha snorted with anger.

"Girlfriend?" came a voice from the doorway, and Gin marched into the room, freshly showered and looking gorgeous in combat shorts and a crisp white tank top. She crackled with energy, immediately focusing on the papers in Solley's hands.

"I barely know her," Solley bleated.

"That's not what I saw out there on the dunes," Janie said in disgust.

Absolutely dumbfounded, Gin turned to Solley for clarification. "What did your sister see?"

"Nothing…something she misinterpreted." Catching Janie's reaction, Solley demanded, "What? What are you implying with your rolling eyes and…and everything?"

Janie left her to fume. Slapping another paper open at a beautiful shot of Solley in her bikini top, she said, "Slut."

"Ooh," Solley cooed, momentarily distracted. She recognized one of the ream of photos Sniper had taken yesterday afternoon out on the dunes. "I look like a model."

Gin glared at her. "When did she take that one?"

Solley always thought that attack was the best means of defense at times like this. Seizing the high ground, she said, "You, of all people, should know better than to believe everything you see in a newspaper. I gave you the benefit of the doubt when you said you haven't slept with all those other women."

"Other?" Janie turned the word over thoughtfully.

"I told you," Marsha informed her, while rolling her eyes at Gin in halfhearted apology.

With a smug little grin, Janie began reading the article aloud. "Kelly Rose should know better than to loosen her tight leash on 'close friend' Gin Ito. The mystery woman seen at Gin's side during filming this week is thought to be a former *Playboy* model and now suburban mom—" She broke off, casting an accusatory look at Solley. "*Playboy*? You never told me—"

"Because it never happened." Solley stated the obvious. "That's bullshit. They're just making it up."

She tried to meet Gin's eyes, to reassure her, but Gin looked away. *What's her fucking problem?* Solley thought. It wasn't as if she'd dragged Sniper down to the beach and said, "Hey, would ya shoot me making out with my secret lover, and while you're at it slap it all over the national papers on the eve of my custody fight." Ms. But-I'm-a-Samurai, with her great career and her groupies and awards, didn't know what a real problem was.

"Wait, there's more." Janie flipped the page.

The explosive banner read, IT'S HOT HOT HOT ON THE BEACH! Solley's blood ran cold, then hot, hot, hot. Two photos jumped out at her. The first was atmospherically shot due to lack of light. It featured her and Gin on the moonlit deck the first time they'd kissed. Gin was flat on her back, her beautiful profile raised in ecstasy to the moon, her back arched and her shirt unbuttoned. Solley was draped over her, head buried in her naked torso. There was no doubt that she was kissing Gin's breasts, even if they couldn't be seen directly through the curtain of her hair. The image was so erotic it looked staged. *Another one for the porno sites,* she thought glumly. When would this misery end?

The second photo showed Gin perched on the top railing of the veranda, looking incredibly roguish with a beer bottle in one hand and the other wedged in the panty line of a smiling Solley. She simpered at the handsome stunt woman as she happily accepted the grope. *Oh, shit. I do look like a concubine.*

"You trollop," Janie spluttered.

"I knew you guys were getting it on." Marsha laughed. She had the audacity to try a high five with Gin.

Looking too stunned to reciprocate, Gin said, "Oh, my God. She's been spying on us."

"No kidding." Solley's face burned with shame.

"Well, I hope you're enjoying turning my home into a brothel." Janie harangued her. "Just how many fucks have you been enjoying on your quote unquote family holiday for rest and recuperation?"

"Don't you dare talk to me like that in front of my children," Solley cried. Though they were well out of earshot, she thought she'd play the moral indignation card.

"*Now* you're worried about your kids?" Janie shook the paper vehemently at her. "Open your eyes and look at the paper. It's a bit late to worry now."

The shrill of the phone added to the general alarm. Solley automatically reached out, if only to stop its incessant ringing.

"Don't. It'll be the press." Marsha said.

But it was too late. The phone was at Solley's ear.

"Hello, Rayner-Bren residence," she said. "Can I help you?"

"Yes, Solley. You can tell me why my children are in chunks and the Karate Kid has her hand in my wife's pants," demanded Dan.

CHAPTER ELEVEN

Dan's Beemer had no sooner glided to a halt before the veranda when the kids bounded down to greet her, squealing in excitement. Solley hung back on the steps with an anxious Janie.

"I've got a broken wrist," Jed announced.

"Sharks nearly ate me." Della raised her arms and nestled into Dan, who swung her into a tight hug.

Will pointed to his patch. "I've only one eye."

"I can do stunts," Jed boasted. "Gin showed me how."

Will continued the litany of carnage. "Aunt Marsha fell off a Jet Ski. She's got gangrene."

"Can Nelson come and live with us?" Della begged. "Please."

"Well, that all sounds lovely," Dan drawled. "I'm so glad you're having such a great holiday with your mother and Aunt Janie." Her cool blue eyes locked with Solley's. "Hello, sweetheart."

Moving onto the veranda, she leaned down and kissed Solley slowly and deliberately on the cheek, ensuring she had enough time to breathe in her scent and feel the heat of her lips.

From the shady depths of her bedroom balcony, Gin

watched the kiss with a queasy stomach. She wished she'd gone to the film shoot with Marsha, who'd wisely removed herself for the day, saying her problems with Dan's attitude got the better of her. She told Gin she didn't want to say anything that might upset the kids.

Gin had planned to keep a low profile. It made her nauseous to think of Dan arriving to reclaim her position at the center of her children's universe. But for some unfathomable, masochistic reason, she still found herself unobtrusively watching the arrival. She decided her actions were honorable. If Dan got nasty and upset Solley, she would intervene. After all, this fraught, unscheduled visit was the result of her behavior with Solley and the kids. She wouldn't let Solley suffer the consequences alone.

She couldn't help smiling as Nelson leaped up on the new arrival, leaving paw prints and damp sand on Dan's expensive-looking clothes.

"Get this animal off me." Dan's demand was clearly aimed at Solley. "He's putting dog hair all over my slacks."

"Mommy." Della still vied for attention. "His name is Nelson. Can he come home with us, please? He's my best friend."

"No, he can't come home with us. He's a beach dog and he wouldn't be happy in the city. You should know that."

Della immediately accepted this.

How does she do that? Solley wondered for the millionth time. Dan only had to say something and the kids accepted it. For Solley, they were all tears and snot and tantrums unless they got their way.

"Hey, Janie. How are you doing?" Dan finally greeted her sister-in-law. "What, no Marsha in the welcoming party?"

"She knew you were coming and had to go and throw herself off something," Janie deadpanned. "Ain't she the lucky one," was added sotto voce, but Dan chose to ignore her.

"We need to talk." Her eyes drilled into Solley's. "I have a few…concerns."

Solley was tall at five-nine, but Dan was a well-built six-footer. She easily overshadowed Solley, making her feel at a disadvantage. Automatically, she brushed a paw mark off Dan's raw linen jacket. "You didn't need to come all the way out here. We could have dealt with this on the phone."

Picking up on Solley's tension, as she always did, Janie drew her car keys from her pocket. "Come on, kids. I'm heading into town for cheesecake. Who wants to come along? We can bring some back for your mommies."

It was an easy bribe and as the kids piled into her car with Nelson, Janie met Solley's eyes and mouthed "good luck" in solidarity.

"Shall we?" Dan gestured toward the house.

Entering the coolness of the darkened hallway, she hesitated for a second and raised her eyes to the upstairs balcony, where Gin stood ramrod straight, arms crossed over a muscular chest, biceps bulging with tension, jaw firm and eyes enigmatic. Solley caught her breath as Dan's icy stare locked with Gin's and a flicker of cold contempt flashed between the two. She could see that Dan sensed the raw power and anger of the smaller woman and probably had no doubt that she could leap from that height and cheerfully throttle her given half the chance. With a blaze of blue hatred she continued after Solley.

Gin sighed aloud and leaned back against the wall. Boy, but Danielle Vitelli was one arrogant motherfucker, exactly as Marsha had described her. Gin's heart ached over the joy the children had displayed on seeing their absent parent. *You don't deserve them, you freakishly tall bitch.* With that white-hot thought, she grabbed her car keys. She had to leave the house before she imploded with jealousy, resentment, and outright rage. How had Solley ended up with that cold monster for a partner? Within seconds of greeting Dan, her vibrancy had dimmed as though a cloud had moved over her. Her body language, usually so full and effervescent, became muted and compressed. She looked colorless, almost unrecognizable as the sexy, passionate woman Gin had made love with the night before.

Gin strode downstairs with single-minded purpose. She had to escape before she burst into the family room and yanked Solley out of there and away from Dan forever.

❖

"So." Dan sat on the smooth leather couch, one long leg elegantly crossed over the other. "It seems you've been busy."

"Not that it's any of your business."

"The minute my kids hit the tabloid headlines it became my business," Dan snapped.

They sat in terse silence for a moment.

"So, where's Trixie?" Solley asked with phony innocence. "I'd have thought she'd be sucking this up, trying to milk it for all it's worth. A tenuous connection with a celebrity could promote her porn-stroke-modeling career."

Dan flicked a cool, scornful look her way. "Jealousy looks so clichéd on redheads."

Solley bristled at the casual put-down. "Excuse me, I'm auburn haired, and I'm not jealous of that skinny bitch."

"You're hell on heels, is what you are," Dan bit back at her. Relaxing again, she repositioned the conversation. "Anyway, I haven't seen Trixie in a while. She's moved to Miami."

Solley mulled this new information over. "Are you going to follow her?"

"It seems unlikely." With a look of utmost distaste, Dan

brushed a dog hair from her pant leg. "Something has opened up here, a deal I can probably land. It's a good opportunity and it's local. It would set me up for several more years on the West Coast."

Dan owned a digital special effects company and relied on contracts from the LA studios. Originally, she'd planned the move east to follow up several options after a lucrative TV commercial deal. Solley wasn't sure how she felt, listening to Dan open the door once more for them as a family. If she'd really shelved the crazy notion of taking the children away for part of the year, she'd just lifted an incredible burden off Solley's shoulders. Now no matter what happened in court, if Dan stayed in California, Solley would be nearby. And if Trixie was truly out of the picture, maybe Dan would turn her full attention back on her kids and really think about what was best for them.

"So you're staying?" Solley asked

"I decided it would be better for the kids. Less upheaval." Dan contemplated the toe of one immaculate loafer. "So I'm investigating this new opportunity. I need to set up finance and take a look at the legal issues. But for now, I'm staying." Her eyes narrowed. "Needless to say, it's not helpful to have pictures of my wife whoring around with some bungee-jumping wannabe-butch splashed all over the papers. Cuckolding doesn't sit well with my Armani business suits."

"You have some nerve talking about cuckolding, with your track record. And you know damn well that was a paparazzi setup."

"Oh, yeah. You just happened to fall forward, mouth first, onto her naked chest. Happens all the time."

"It happened to you whenever Trixie showed up. Though God knows, you didn't have to fall very far onto those silicone hillocks, did you?"

Another terse silence.

"This is getting us nowhere." Dan took a breath and seemed to consciously curb her sarcasm. "I'm not here for us to scratch each other's eyes out over our…meaningless flirtations."

"Meaningless? Last time we talked, you wanted your bimbo to be stepmother of our kids for six months of each year."

"I've just told you it's in the past. I'm here to help with what's left of the kids after the shark attacks and who knows what else. I trust you've been keeping all the pieces in a bag for reattachment later."

"They were dolphins, and don't play the perfect parent with me. If it had been you and Trixie on the beach that day, Della would have sailed to Hawaii by now."

"Let it go," Dan warned. "I'm willing to overlook your public sex acts with that stuntwoman, but I want to know how the kids were injured. That's why I drove out here. I was worried."

Solley sighed. This was going to be the hard part, explaining the run of events over the past few days. "Well, what you saw in the papers was misleading. They're actually having an incredible vacation. Gin being here has just blown them away." Oops, bad choice of words. She continued quickly. "We've had a few minor incidents, that's all."

Dan wasn't willing to settle for the abridged version. "What happed to Jed?"

"He saw Gin leap off Janie's balcony one day and tried to copy her."

"For God's sake, he could have broken his neck."

"Gosh, I never thought of that."

"What about Will?"

"He was playing in her trailer and stuck a makeup pencil in his eye. Thought he was Johnny Depp or something."

"He was in her trailer, unsupervised?"

"Not for long, and he only wears that patch because he likes it."

"Hmm." Dan didn't sound impressed. "It sounds like they've been spending far too much time around your friend Gin Ito."

Trying not to sound defensive, Solley said, "We have Gin to thank for rescuing Della when she floated out too far on her bodyboard."

"Wonderful, she's a hero. But what were the twins doing with bodyboards? They're far too young." As usual, Dan seemed to be looking for any excuse to escalate her criticism. "Why the hell did you buy them? I suppose they whined and you caved in, as usual."

"Actually, they were a gift from Gin."

"Oh, I see." Dan sneered. "She's had a hand in everything, hasn't she?" She looked pointedly at Solley's shorts.

Flushing with anger, Solley avoided the angry blue eyes. "This is not about Gin. As I said, the kids are doing fine, and they really needed to have some fun after all they've been put through recently."

She waited for Dan to react to the dig, but her face was impassive.

In a soft, conciliatory tone, she asked, "So, where do we go from here?" She touched Solley's arm.

❖

Rather than endure an awkward dinner, Gin decided to dine alone in town. It was much, much later when she finally drove the studio car back to Janie and Marsha's house. As she pulled into the drive, her eyes froze on Dan's Beemer and her heart grew cold. Why was that woman still here?

Carefully, she entered the house. A soft sound came from

the kitchen, the clicking of the refrigerator door. Standing back in the shadows, Gin observed a butt-naked Dan with a glass of water in her hand. She padded upstairs toward Solley's room. After a second, Gin followed, her heart thumping painfully in her chest with an erratic, panicked rhythm.

A shaft of light across the hall drew her eyes like a magnet to Solley's partially open bedroom door. Dan and Solley stood naked beside the bed in a soft, intimate embrace. Their kissing was tender. Dan stroked her fingers idly along the planes of Solley's back until, hands on her shoulders, she slowly pushed her down to sit on the edge of the bed. As she descended under the pressure of Dan's palms, Solley gently left a trail of kisses all the way down Dan's flat stomach to the shaved pubic mound. While she was distracted and unaware of their voyeur, Dan turned her head and stared squarely, with absolutely no emotion, into Gin's eyes.

Gin stood frozen in the hallway, stricken by the tenderness and devotion Solley was lavishing on this cold, cold woman. Never breaking eye contact, Dan lifted her arm and lazily swung the door closed in Gin's face.

Shame and humiliation swept over Gin in a heated and hateful rush. Dan had known she was there, in the kitchen. She knew Gin had followed her. And she wanted her to see this, to see how much Solley still loved her.

❖

As they moved closer on the bed, Dan nuzzled Solley's neck. Usually she loved this move, but now it was tickly and annoying.

"Don't leave a mark," she blurted.

Dan raised her head and looked at her, slightly affronted.

"Sorry," Solley muttered contritely.

Shifting her weight, Dan turned her attention to Solley's breasts, massaging them, mashing them together, remembering Solley liked to play rough.

"Ouch. No. They're too tender."

Dan stiffened and stopped, momentarily uncertain. Solley wrapped her arms around her neck and slid her thigh between Dan's legs, nudging against her sex. Accepting their tired old standby position, Dan moved against her. It never failed. She climaxed quickly and relaxed into Solley's embrace, burying her face in Solley's hair.

Solley stroked along her shoulders and down her back, tightening her arms when she felt Dan try to move.

"Shh," she whispered, wanting to avoid the next phase, the one where she would have to let Dan touch her and appear aroused when she wasn't. "Just let me hold you."

They lay there in the dark, in a silence that seemed sad and empty. Tracing small, meandering circles on Dan's body, Solley stared at the ceiling. They couldn't get it back. They never would.

As though sensing the emotional void between them and finding it an unwelcome bed companion, Dan stood and stretched her long, well-toned body. Solley took in her familiar, still pleasing frame. It was so different from Gin's. The thought appeared from nowhere. It was funny how she'd never made a comparison before. Gin's body was small and tight and very sexy, with loads of muscles.

I've had Dan as a partner for years. But as a lover? Well, not for a long time. And now, in one week, here she was with two lovers to compare, an old one and a new one. And the way she felt about them was so different. Dan was...comfortable. Like an old shoe, one that could still cause a blister. Their passion had well and truly gone. They were just going through the motions. It was quite sad, really. After all this time, they couldn't find the spark that had once ignited so easily between them.

She was glad they'd tried again. For themselves as a couple, for their family, and if only to prove something to herself. Now she knew. They both knew. It was over.

But with Gin. My God, the energy she gave and demanded in return. Solley felt like some sort of animal when they made love. She smiled weakly. She craved the touch of Gin's skin and missed her when they were apart. Despite her intense sexual awareness of Gin, she also felt comfortable and safe with her. Gin seemed to accept her exactly as she was. She genuinely seemed to like her. Solley couldn't remember the last time she'd felt that from a lover. She wasn't sure if she'd *ever* felt liked or respected by Dan.

When this was all over, she hoped Gin would still want to see her. A glum thought intruded. Who knew where they would all be after this vacation? Gin could be anywhere in the world, with anybody. She would be surrounded by bloodsuckers like Kelly Rose, all clamoring for a piece of her.

With a sigh, Solley hopped out of bed and followed Dan to the bathroom. She was a fool to think of including Gin in her future, even in her wildest daydreams.

CHAPTER TWELVE

T hat is one blackhearted bitch." Gin fumed as she pulled out a chair at the kitchen table and set her morning coffee down. "I could sense her lack of pulse from a hundred yards. She's like Lurch with a ponytail."

Marsha studied her from over the rim of her cup. "Maybe you didn't notice, but she's a blackhearted, no-pulse *butch* with a capital *B*. Maybe the Rayner women like 'em strong and tall."

Gin shot her a venomous look. Sometimes the jibes about her height wore thin, and she was in no mood for smug, six-foot brunettes today. "The family resemblance is amazing. You both look eerily alike, in a good-twin-evil-twin kind of way."

"Yeah, the sexy twin and the Lurch twin. I don't know what Janie ever saw in Dan, but since she was the one who introduced us I can't complain."

"I'd rather not think about Dan being with two Rayner sisters." Gin wrinkled her nose. "Eew, that's practically incest."

"And when did you become Judge Judy?" Marsha sniffed.

"When I saw that bitch get out of her car." Gin shook her head, still in disbelief at all she'd witnessed since Dan's arrival. How the hell did someone warm and sweet like Solley end up with that monster?

"I told you to come to the film shoot with me. But no, you had to torture yourself."

"I'm not the type who runs away," Gin said pointedly.

"Really? Last time we talked I thought you were going to run away from Solley as fast as you could. You were going to take no chances, remember? Next thing, there's pornography all over the papers. What's up with that?"

Gin sagged back in her chair with a loud sigh. Staring up at the rotating ceiling fan, she said flatly, "Nothing's going on, Marsh. It was just a summer fling. I can't believe it made the front page of the entertainment section."

"Yeah, real shitty luck. But you have to admit it's pretty funny."

"Are you nuts? There's nothing funny about this situation." Gin scowled. Sometimes she wondered about her best friend's mindset.

"I was talking about Kelly Rose," Marsha huffed, like Gin had missed the whole point. "She's the one who dragged Sniper down here to take steamy pictures, and it totally backfired." She sipped her latte with satisfaction. "Way to go, Kelly. Not just a dumb blonde, but a national idiot, too."

"You're no help at all."

"When did you fall hook, line, and sinker for Solley, by the way?"

Gin avoided her eyes. "Is it that obvious?"

Marsha shrugged. "I put it down to the parenting gene. Maybe we fall for people we can raise a family with. Maybe it's as basic as that. I mean, that's how it works in the natural world." She looked impressed with her own theory.

"Do you think this has fucked up Solley's chances for custody?" Gin asked.

"Royally," Marsha replied confidently. "It's just the

opening Dan was waiting for. Solley's going to have to suck up big time if she wants to see her kids."

Gin laid her head on her arms on the table top. She recalled her insistence to Solley about wanting only the best for her and the kids. Hollow words now. Solley had worried that their attraction would fuck things up for her, and she was right. *I've ruined it all, me and my media circus.*

"The thing about Lurch," Marsha continued, warming to her nemesis cousin's new nickname, "is she's very shrewd and manipulative. That's why she's such a good businesswoman. You know Ego FX? That's her company."

Gin raised her head. She recognized the name. Ego FX was a small, studio-supported business with a good reputation for special effects software. She stared past Marsha, strangely aware of cogs and wheels starting to spin.

Rising, she said, "I have some things to organize. Catch you later, Marsha."

She stepped out onto the veranda and absorbed the bay views for several long seconds. She felt so at peace in this little cove—it was her karmic cradle—and she just knew the pieces of her life would come together here. First, however, she had some important things to take care of. She hadn't met with her accountant for almost a year. It was time they had a conversation.

❖

Dan was silent throughout the drive to the restaurant. She'd insisted they have breakfast alone so that they could "talk." Solley wondered what on earth she had to say that took such staging.

When they'd finally settled into their booth and placed their order, Dan said, "Solley, I want to discuss our future."

"Didn't we do that yesterday?"

"Not really. I wanted to tell you some more about the deal I'm considering." When Solley didn't respond like a cheerleader, she said, "I thought it mattered to you that the kids would still be close by when they're with me."

"Of course. I don't want them disappearing for half the year to God knows where."

Dan shifted uncomfortably. "Well, that's the outside option now that Trixie and I are no longer together. Though I suppose I could still pick up business back east." She paused as their food arrived. "But I'm going to concentrate on getting this deal signed. Like I said, it suits everyone if I stay here."

Solley smeared her pancake stack with whipped butter. "Yes, it'll be great if the kids don't have to pay for our separation by being dragged from one school to the next every six months. That would be appalling." She ladled on some more guilt, since it obviously hadn't occurred to Dan to think about the consequences of her actions. "Imagine how far behind they'd be by the time they reached high school."

"That's exactly what I was thinking, so I'm making this deal my priority." Dan's eyes burned into hers. "I've raised half a million, but I need twice that amount. The total output is going to be approximately a million for me, but it will start to pay back a percentage almost immediately."

Solley was confused. Dan didn't usually talk money with her. A germ of suspicion formed in her mind and she asked, "Are you planning to extend the mortgage on our house?"

Dan's faint, unapologetic smile said it had already been done. She was the one who took care of their material life as a couple. Solley concentrated on being the mother and homemaker.

"I have something else in mind to raise the rest of the capital." Dan shifted again, and Solley could feel the crunch coming. From the leaden feeling in her stomach, she knew she wasn't going to like whatever Dan was hatching.

"If we were to stay together for the kids' sake, we could turn a blind eye to each other's…adventures outside the relationship. I mean, after last night we've proven we can do that."

"You're suggesting we have an open relationship?" Solley asked dryly. "Only this time it's not one-sided. We both see other people?"

"Why not? I can accept that we've evolved toward nonmonogamy over the years. You could continue to see the Karate Kid, if that's what you want, but we'd stay together for the children's sake."

Solley was stunned. This wasn't what she'd hoped to hear. Dan had behaved as if their relationship was unofficially "open" practically since Solley had come home from the hospital with the twins. Sometimes she'd felt that her heart lived on an arid prairie, so "open" was their life together that tumbleweed blew through it. But she didn't want their relationship to be exclusive; she simply didn't want it at all.

Dan continued, oblivious to Solley's stiff shoulders and the scornful reply that hovered on her lips. "Of course, for this to work out the way we both want I need the extra cash." Her eyes glittered cold, bright blue. "So, considering the traumatic experience our kids have been put through over the past two weeks, I thought we should consult a lawyer."

"You're going to make this a custody issue? A few scrapes on a summer vacation? The judge will laugh at you."

Dan bestowed a patronizing smile on her. "No, I'm going to discuss what amount would be an appropriate settlement for Ms. Ito's role in the physical endangerment and psychological trauma of our children."

Shocked, Solley said, "They're not traumatized, they're thrilled. This is crazy."

"No, this is a lawsuit." Dan grinned like a hyena with a brand new carcass to pull apart. "Don't get yourself worked up on Ito's behalf. She can afford it."

"That's not the point."

"I had a feeling you wouldn't go for it. You've never been able to see the financial opportunities lurking within life's stinky moments. You just don't have the smarts or the balls to take advantage."

"If you mean there are some things I won't sink to, then yes, you're right."

Dan held up a hand with patient amusement. "Okay. Here's plan B. Tell Ito I'm going to sue her but if she were to cough up the investment I need, not only would she and her movie have no more adverse publicity, but the kids would stay here. And, of course, you two could see each other."

Solley could see she truly believed she was being magnanimous. "That's blackmail."

"No, it's business. I need the money and you've provided a means of getting it." She played her proud parent ace card. "I'm trying to do the right thing by us here, Sol. I want my company to grow from strength to strength, so we're financially secure. I want my kids to go to the best colleges, and drive preppie cars, and have gap years in Europe."

"Bullshit," Solley snapped. "Don't give me that crap about how much you care for the kids. You don't give a damn about anyone but yourself and your fucking deal. You just use everybody. You're a jerk."

"I'm the jerk who writes the checks," Dan corrected in a patronizing tone. "It's just as well one of us is thinking about the future."

"Gin loves the kids and they love her back."

"That's exactly what I'm talking about. And she seems

to care for you. So she can pay up and keep you and the kids close, or be sued and named in a bitter custody battle…not good publicity on the eve of a massive launch of a family movie. She's not stupid. I'm sure she'll do the smart thing."

"It's blackmail, any way you look at it. You can go to hell."

"God, you're dense. The money we need is a piddling amount to her. She probably spends that every year on shoes."

"I'll tell you what I'm going to do," Solley said. "I'm going to sue for full custody as the biological mother."

"No, you're not. After this week's little fiasco any good lawyer will be able to paint you as the unfit mother you are. Unable to care for your kids because you're so wrapped up in some *macha* stunt queen." Dan got to her feet. "Think about it carefully, Solley. But be quick. Those pictures of you and Ito are already plastered all over the Internet and not on the most discerning of sites, either, catch my drift? That's not going to look good at a custody hearing, now, is it?" With that, she swooped angrily from the restaurant.

Solley couldn't believe Dan would use her family this way, as a lever to blackmail a person whose only mistake was to care about them. *But I can believe she stuck me with the bill. And I've no way home. Bitch!*

❖

"Play daddy with my kids and fuck my wife?" Dan ground out between tight lips as she stalked into the kitchen. "You little pissant, we'll see who gets fucked."

"Did you say something?" Janie stepped out from behind the fridge door.

"Where's the home wrecker?" Dan swung her brilliant blue gaze toward the stairs.

Cocking her head and feigning a confused frown, Janie replied, "Aren't I looking at her?"

Dan shrugged off the jibe, offering her own sharp retort. "Remind me, why did we ever date?"

"Good question." Janie poured several glasses of juice for the children. "Gin's in her room. If you're planning to cause trouble, I suggest you think about the fact that your kids are in the family room and will hear everything."

"Let me worry about what's appropriate for my family." Dan headed for the stairs.

"Where's Solley?" Janie glanced out the open door.

"She'll be back later," Dan said tersely. "Thanks for minding the kids, by the way. I thought it was important to patch things up with your sister so we could stay together."

She lifted her gaze, and Janie noticed a pair of legs and Gin's large duffel bags at the top of the stairs.

"Going somewhere?" Dan sounded smug.

"Yes."

"Do you have a minute before you head out?"

"I do, but I was planning to spend it with the children. To say good-bye."

Gin's voice was so strained, Janie thought about intervening. Dan's height and bullying tactics didn't intimidate her, but she wanted to avoid a scene. There was enough stress in the house.

"Gin has to get to the airport," she said weakly.

"We can take a quick walk." Gin picked up the bags and started down the stairs.

Retreating, Dan said, "I'll wait on the veranda."

After she'd exited the kitchen, Janie met Gin's eyes. "I wish you would stay."

"It's better for everyone if I don't. It sounds like Dan is attempting to keep their family together."

"I wonder how long that'll last." Janie hesitated. "You don't have to talk to her. All she wants to do is make you feel bad."

Gin dropped the bags beside the door with a rueful smile. "Nothing she says could make this any worse."

"I wouldn't bet on that." Less than convinced by Dan's claim about that she and Solley were going to stay together, Janie said, "Please, Gin. Delay your flight till tomorrow so you can see Solley before you go."

"I expected to see her now, but perhaps it's better that she isn't here." Gin slipped her arm around Janie's waist. "This situation is a mess and I'm responsible for my part in that. The least I can do is step back and let them work things out."

Janie wished she knew what Dan and Solley had talked about during their private breakfast. She had trouble believing Solley would just walk right back into the relationship that had made her so unhappy. Nothing was going to change. But Gin was right. It was probably better that she kept her distance.

The thought made Janie sad. She'd seen how Solley glowed around Gin, and how Gin came alive when they were together. Giving Gin a squeeze, she said, "Sometimes the timing isn't right. But that can change. Nothing stands still."

Gin sighed. "Tell Solley I'm sorry I missed her."

"Did you try her cell phone?" Janie could hear a note of desperation in her own voice.

"Yes, and I heard it ringing in her room."

"Goddamn," Janie muttered. Dan only had to snap her fingers and Solley jumped to. She'd seemed flustered when they left and had obviously forgotten her phone in the rush not to keep Dan waiting.

"It's okay," Gin said. "Just tell her I'll be thinking of her and I hope everything works out the way she wants."

Janie's throat was too thick for her to form a reply. As she watched Gin walk out the door, she felt a sense of helpless gloom. Solley had to make her own mistakes, but Janie had a feeling this would be one of her biggest.

❖

Solley pounded into the trailer camp several hours later and realized she had no idea where Gin or Marsha were working today. They were usually out on location somewhere around the bay, but where? She plucked idly at a waist-high stem of blackened dune grass and whipped it before her as she walked. Maybe if she went directly to Gin's trailer? She paused, gazing around for someone to ask about today's shoot. Two young women walked nonchalantly past her, slipping sly sideways glances in her direction before lowering their heads.

"That's her," one whispered loudly to the other. "She's a professional dominatrix Ito had flown in from Rio."

Solley groaned. It was those two gossiping bitches again. Did their entire job involve waltzing up and down this trailer park, talking absolute shit? Slivers of their conversation drifted toward her.

"A dominatrix? You have got to be kidding me. Not with those looks. I heard she's a fan. Some crazy stalker."

"And I heard Kelly Rose has fluid on her lungs and might die."

"I wish."

"She has her own BDSM porn site," the friend insisted. "It's called Rayner Terror."

"Don't look now, but I think she's following us."

They both threw cautious glances over their shoulders and paled to see Solley bearing down on them like a dungeon mistress ready to whoop some ass. She'd heard more than enough of their vacuous bitching. They took to their heels, scrambling up and over the sand dunes. Mildly stunned by their extreme reaction, Solley dropped her grass "whip" and didn't bother to follow. *Rayner Terror*. She grinned.

She heard her name and turned around to see Marsha striding toward her. "I was looking for you."

"Likewise." Solley looked past Marsha's shoulder. There was no sign of Gin. "I thought I'd find Gin with you. I really need to talk to her."

Marsha's face stilled. "Oh, you missed her, Sol. She just left. She's starting a job in Canada next week."

"Canada? She didn't say anything about that."

"Well that's an international stunt star for you. Gin picks up work anywhere, anytime." Marsha held up a selection of packages she had cradled in her arms. "She asked me to give these to the kids. Plus some extra stuff from the movie…as promised." She fussed with the bags, probably so she didn't have to look at Solley.

Solley was stunned. It was understandable for Gin to have to pack up and move quickly on to the next job. God knew, she'd always expected it to happen. But now that it had she felt the loss so deeply she didn't know how to react.

"She didn't say good-bye." The moment the words left her lips she felt stupid and childish, glad Marsha was looking anywhere but at her.

"She wanted to. But you weren't around. I think she left a message on your cell phone." Marsha tried to console her. She offered an elbow for Solley to link on as they walked back home. "Once she and Dan got through talking, she left right away."

"Dan talked to her?" Solley felt sick. She could imagine how *that* conversation went. No wonder Gin hadn't waited around to exchange fond farewells.

"Guess what?" Marsha made an obvious attempt to lighten

the mood. "There's a cast party at our house next week. For the end of the shoot. Grace is coming down for it."

"That's good." Solley tried her best to sound interested that the youngest Rayner sister was expected, but she fell short of the mark. She was barely listening. Instead she was lost in self-recrimination, her gaze on the distant horizon.

She'd tried to be brave by acting on her attraction to Gin, but her selfish choices had set Gin up for a mean-spirited lawsuit, and now she couldn't even tell her, in person, how dreadfully sorry she was. Or that she wished her good luck for the future. Or that she cared for her and would miss her. Or… *Don't go there, Rayner. You're a fool. Gin doesn't need you. She needs to get far away from you and your miserable mess of a life, and that's exactly what she's doing.*

"Here, can you take these packages back to the house?" Marsha asked. "I gotta go collect Janie's dry cleaning."

The request shook Solley out of her semistupor. She was so close to tears she felt like a teenager. Knowing her distress must be obvious, she said, "Let me run into town instead. I need a little time away."

"Sure." Marsha nodded rapidly. "I'll tell Janie you'll be late for lunch."

"Thanks." With a grateful smile Solley headed back the way she'd come.

She needed time away from the house, if only to compose herself. The more it sank in that Gin had gone, the deeper it cut. There was no way she could face Dan at the moment and not hit her with one of Janie's tasteful ornaments. She had to get away. In fact, she had to break away.

❖

Gin stood like an automaton, shouldering her hand luggage, barely registering the boarding announcement for her flight to Vancouver. Part of her was glad to shuffle toward the gate that would take her away from this hiatus in her numb, empty life. The rest of her screamed in protest, urging her to run from the terminal and kick and scratch and fight for what she wanted. What she needed, to survive as a fully functional human being.

She had known it would be hard to leave, but she still felt betrayed by her feelings. She had so underestimated the dictates of her heart. So much for the sanctuary of La Sirena Verde as a place to heal. Just when she sensed she was finally coming to terms with the loss of Miki, a fresh wound had opened. She felt incredibly fragile at the thought of not seeing Solley again. She felt flayed. Totally raw. Every nerve lay exposed. The pain shocked her, hitting her full force on the chest as though her heart had been ripped apart.

Gin stowed her bags and belted herself into her seat. The image of Dan and Solley together haunted her. What she really needed was a run along La Sirena's cliff tops to shake off her emotional upheaval. Instead she would be trapped in her seat listening to the whine of the engines as her plane took her farther away from any hope she'd ever had of…of what?

She closed her eyes for take-off. Solley's bright smile lit up the darkness, her green gaze dancing with happiness as they sat and watched the seals out in the bay. She'd been so relaxed that day, during those hours they'd spent by themselves for the first time. Gin knew Solley had also felt the connection between them. They couldn't resist each other, although they'd both tried.

Later, when they became lovers, Gin saw a different light in Solley's eyes. Dark and sensual. Bruised with passion. She'd fallen into those eyes and still hadn't emerged. Marsha had warned her of love like this. Love that swallowed you whole. Gin understood her meaning exactly. She'd fallen into Solley, heart and soul.

Her mind wandered full circle to the question she'd been avoiding all day, the pathetic, half-assed question of a hopeless dreamer. Could she manage to woo Solley Rayner away from Dan? It seemed impossible now that they were reunited. Dan was a hard-hearted, self-centered, womanizing pig, but she was still Solley's partner and coparent. During their brief, uncomfortable discussion, Dan had made it clear that she intended to continue in that role.

Gin knew she should be angry and outraged over the proposition Dan put to her, but she felt only a dull sorrow and something close to relief. If she could do something to help Solley, the details weren't important. Knowing how determined Solley was to keep her family together and make sure her kids were happy, it wasn't surprising that she'd decided to try again with her partner. Ultimately it was her choice.

But did she even know she had a choice? Gin had disappeared like a coward, leaving her to draw her own conclusions. What a fool. Why had she not been braver and explained how she felt? Why was she so goddamned scared? She bitterly regretted running away. She should have stayed and fought Dan for her. If Solley refused, it could be no worse than what she felt right now.

Gin had a contract to sign and a location to approve in Vancouver. It would take four days. After that she was free for a month. Once she'd taken care of the other business matters that needed her attention, what would she do? She stared out the window at a cloudless blue sky and, for several long, painful seconds, pictured Solley vanishing from her life forever. She couldn't allow that to happen.

I'm going to give myself a second chance. Because after Miki, this is my second chance at life and love. Perhaps my only one. Please let Solley want a second chance, too.

CHAPTER THIRTEEN

Five days later, Solley paused her SUV at the crest of La Sirena Verde and let the motor idle while she gazed down into the secluded bay, watching the white surf break onto the sun-drenched beach. Gulls swooped and soared idly in the lazy heat of the late afternoon, their haunting cries carried on the wind. The peace and tranquility was a soothing balm for her tattered nerves and crushed spirit.

To her left, far down in the dunes she could see the partially dismantled movie camp. Filming had finally wrapped up and the circus would soon be on its way. Marsha's friends and quite a few of the cast and crew were staying for the party on Saturday. After the farewells, La Sirena Verde would be a haven of tranquility once more. Solley smiled, thinking how relieved Janie would be. No matter how lucrative the deal, she would be glad to get her beach back.

Solley, too, was glad these few weeks of mayhem were officially over. It had been a strange and eventful summer vacation for her. A summer love and a new outlook on her life had turned her and Dan's world upside down. But she had made her decision and had spent the past five days drumming it into a stupefied Dan that she did not want to start over or try again. That though they had children to love and raise, they did not have to emotionally cripple each other.

Solley would be a good mother to their children, but now she wanted that divorce that had hung over her head for far too long. Between them they would look after their children, prioritize them, and do only what was best for them. And to start off as she meant to go on, she had promptly told Dan to take a turn parenting full time while Solley stayed at La Sirena Verde to help Janie prepare for a cast party and to spend time with her little sister Grace.

She had even packed the kids' clothing and thrown their bags into the trunk of Dan's car, ignoring her protests. Since Dan knew so much about being a good parent and keeping their family safe, Solley figured it was time for her to translate talk into action. She and Janie had hysterics as Dan drove away, outnumbered and outmaneuvered.

Recalling her panicked face, Solley chuckled. She'd had five days all to herself for the first time since Jed was born, and she was never going back to being the frazzled, exhausted mother of three who'd arrived in Topaz Bay three weeks earlier. It was time to reclaim herself—the Solley who had seemed absent for so long she had almost vanished entirely.

With a slightly teary smile, she listened again to the voicemail message she'd saved. "Solley, I don't want to say good-bye, so it's good that you're not here. Whatever happens, you can trust that I care for you and the children and I always will. I hope you find what you're looking for."

Gin's words soothed her and thrilled her and made her feel that anything was possible. Solley had thought about rushing to Vancouver as soon as Dan and the kids drove away, but she'd decided to take some time and clear her mind of all the crap and chaos. She didn't believe that her feelings for Gin were some kind of rebound reaction, but she needed to be certain of herself before she saw Gin again. And she would see her again, no matter what. She owed herself that much.

Feeling at peace for the first time in years, she rolled on down into the bay, heading for Janie's house.

❖

Shortly after Janie and Solley had prepared and served up a simple meal outdoors, a beat-up old Jeep came hurtling down the hill, throwing up a plume of dust and grit behind it. The style of driving, rather than the vehicle, announced the visitor.

"Hey, Gracie's getting a little better at the ole timekeeping lark. She's here early," Solley observed wryly.

"But always in time for a meal," Janie said. "I guess that's her gift in this life."

"Yeah, that and pulling teeth. No surprises there," Marsha muttered darkly.

The old Jeep skidded to a gravelly halt beside Solley's car. The door was kicked open and the youngest of the Rayner sisters jumped out. She bounded up to the deck to be enthusiastically hugged by her siblings. Visually, she was a variation on the family theme, blond like Janie but with mischievous brown eyes rather than the flashing green of her sisters. Height-wise, she fell somewhere between the two. Temper-wise, she was way out there with Solley, but she had a healthy share of Janie's shrewdness, too.

"My, it's like the new season of *Charmed*," Marsha remarked as the sisters fell into a group hug. "Or maybe *Macbeth*."

"Get your bags, Gracie, and I'll fix you a plate of food," Janie ordered, pausing as she noticed the vast collection of bags and boxes piled up in the back of the Jeep. "How long were you actually planning on staying?"

Grace shuffled slightly. "Well, a little longer than the

weekend. I've been kicked out of school. I'll need to look around to see where I can complete my degree. But in the meantime I'm taking the rest of the year off."

Janie and Solley both spoke at once, talking over each other in a gabble of stunned accusation.

"Kicked out of school?"

"What the hell did you do…steal drugs?"

"Push drugs?"

Grace looked miffed at the lack of sibling support. "No, I didn't steal or push drugs. But I *was* caught misappropriating the gas and air, and an articulator…on Debbie Steenson. She got suspended, and now she's not talking to me."

"Do I even want to know what an articulator is?" Solley asked in exasperation.

"Not in this context."

"I can't believe you'd throw away your education for some ditz," Janie scolded, hands on hips.

"Is Debbie Steenson hot?" Marsha wanted to know.

"Lava in a Pop-Tart."

"All right!" Marsha and Grace high-fived, much to Janie and Solley's disgust.

The fallout from this particular bombshell temporarily contained, they moved to the outdoor table and began their evening meal.

"You can start checking out schools online tomorrow, before the rest of the guests arrive," Janie said. "It'll be pretty crowded after that and you'll have no peace until everyone leaves again on Sunday."

"How many are staying over?" Solley asked.

"Well, we've got a pretty full house. Most people are staying down at the camp in the last of the trailers." Janie hesitated, exchanging a glance with Marsha.

"What's the chance of bagging the front guest suite?" Grace chanced her luck. "I hear Gin Ito left already? Bummer."

"Well." Janie shifted awkwardly. "As a matter of fact, Gin's coming back for the party." She darted a quick look at Solley.

"So she'll need her room, kiddo." Marsha, as usual, didn't pick up on the undercurrent and continued chatting spare-bed strategy with Grace.

"When?" Solley's question emerged as a squeak.

"Tonight." Janie gave her a long, pointed look.

Composing her face as much as possible, considering her heart was hammering fit to rupture her chest, Solley rose and excused herself. "I'll go bring in your bags, Grace."

She couldn't get away quickly enough. Her stomach was churning and heat flooded her face. Ducking her head to hide her flaming cheeks from Janie's curious stare, she slid from the room. *Gin's coming back? I'll get to see her again.*

❖

Grace decided to go for a walk after lunch and refresh her memories of her new temporary digs. Good surf, she could use that. Hot sun, she could top up her tan. Long beach, she could get out her running shoes. All she needed was for Debbie Steenson to get over herself, get down here, and get her body over Grace's, preferably butt naked.

Grace smirked to herself. She enjoyed being a player, and college had supplied some easy pickings. *Not too sure who I'll get to play with in this place, though,* she mused wistfully. No sooner had the thought crossed her mind than she crested a sand dune to find a delectably pert khaki bottom and a beautifully muscled nude back on the sand before her. Pausing so as not to alarm the bronzed beach booty she'd found, Grace noted the photographic bag lying to the side and the camera screening the stranger's face. Its massive telephoto lens was pointed across the dunes directly at her sister's house.

Aha, this must be the infamous Sniper Jones, here for the arrival of any celebrity party guests. Apparently she planned to torture the family with more seedy celluloid disclosures. And knowing her family, degenerates that they were, there'd be plenty more of the same. Grace decided she'd better save the day, and have a little fun at the same time. Lord knew when a morsel of such tempting eye candy would pass her way again, out here.

Slithering silently down the dune, she was immediately upon Sniper, twisting the photographer's left lower leg in a fluid aikido movement that would have brought tears of pride to Gin Ito and Marsha Bren. If the yelps were any indication, the move brought tears of pain to Sniper's.

"So it's true. Perps return to the scene of their crime. How tediously predictable but happily accommodating," Grace snapped, applying pressure.

Sniper squealed. "What the fuck? Get off me, you fucking lunatic."

"You know what I'm gonna do? I'm gonna snap your tendon like a cheese straw if you don't watch that potty mouth," Grace snarled, leaning on the limb for emphasis.

Sniper squealed louder. "Okay, Okay. Tell me what you want," she practically sobbed.

"First, I want a piece of your ass, but I haven't yet decided what piece or how I want it. Second, I'm gonna march you down to my sister's house so you can apologize to my family for the media frenzy you created. Did you know my sister Solley has an entire porn site dedicated to her? How do you think that feels?"

"Much, much worse than having your lower leg slowly ripped off. Tell her I'm sorry. I'm so, so sorry. Please, please get off me before I pass out," Sniper howled. "I'll do anything you ask, please stop."

"You'll tell her sorry yourself. And, believe me, you *will* do anything I ask." Letting go of the leg, Grace flipped the exhausted young woman onto her back. She took in the startled and fearful clear gray eyes, the round sand-dusted breasts, and the quivering muscles of her prey's belly, rising and falling with each frightened breath.

"Shit. You're the Rayner I haven't met, aren't you?" Sniper managed to squeak.

"Yeah, three's the magic number," Grace growled. "Who are you working for this time? I heard you were Kelly Rose's hand puppet, but she's dumped you now, hasn't she? Who's your new paymaster?"

"No one. I'm freelancing." She waved her lens in Grace's direction. "I don't suppose—"

"Dare, and the only thing going snap around here will be your neck."

Grace glared at the neck under threat and then let her eyes once again stroll across Sniper's broad, tanned shoulders and down to those sweet little breasts. The nipples immediately hardened, and Grace glanced up. Her eyes locked with an intense, smoky stare. She swallowed hard. So did Sniper.

Grace managed to keep her thoughts in focus, but only just. Sniper's charms were seriously swaying her resolve. "You're gonna come with me and meet the folks, got it?"

Sniper nodded. "Okay, but you also wanted a piece of my ass, didn't you? Is that still to tick off your to-do list?"

Recognizing the invitation for what it was, Grace decided the family meeting could wait. She pushed the hot stranger roughly back onto the sand and kissed the generous lips. "Yeah," she moaned into Sniper's mouth, her hand moving for the photographer's zipper, "let's tick all the boxes."

Frantically they began to peel each other's clothes off.

"I'm glad you like lying round in the sand, 'cos by the

time I've finished with you, we'll have sifted half this beach through our panties," Grace murmured before falling into another kiss.

❖

Solley found Janie slamming round the laundry room, trying to break as many white appliances as humanly possible. She knew her sister was upset. This was classic Janie behavior. If in doubt, wash your best cashmere sweater in boiling water, then cry into the suds.

"Can I talk to you?" she queried apprehensively. She needed a friend, she needed support. She needed her sister.

Janie paused in her strangulation of a fabric softener bottle. "Yes. I think it's about time you did. What's going on, Sol?"

"It's about Gin, but you already know that."

Janie sighed. "I know you're hurting and I know Gin was very upset when she left. You can tell me anything. I promise not to preach."

Solley took a deep breath and plunged in, summarizing the latest crisis in her sorry life. "Dan's trying to sue Gin for all the kids' injuries. At least, she's making threatening noises about it. She thinks she can make Gin cough up enough cash to pull off a deal with a local studio."

"Gin won't fall for that," Janie scoffed. "She'll get a shit-hot attorney and blow Dan out of the water."

"I'm not so sure."

Dan had seemed pretty pleased with herself that day when Solley finally got back to the house. At first, Solly had assumed the satisfaction was at Gin's departure. Now she suspected there was more to it. She'd tried pumping Dan about exactly what was said in her conversation with Gin, to no avail. All she could conclude was that her manipulative ex thought she'd scored some kind of victory.

"Well, Dan can't sue without your help," Janie pointed out. "She wasn't even here when the accidents happened and knows diddly about what went on. If you stick by Gin, Dan won't have a leg to stand on and she knows it."

"That's what she's banking on, that I stick by Gin. Then she'll have a good chance of winning custody because of all the hands-in-knickers publicity."

"God, she's such a snake."

Solley groaned. Her guilt at causing Gin's predicament rolled off her in waves. She felt so stupid for playing into Dan's oily hands. "I don't know what I'm going to say to Gin."

"It's not your fault Dan decided to pull this stunt," Janie said.

"I knew the risks. I knew Dan would play dirty if she found out what was going on here," Solley said miserably. "Being sued would be terrible for Gin's career and the movie, on top of all the paparazzi stuff, so Dan thinks she'll simply pay to make it go away."

She wondered what Gin made of Dan's blackmail. Did she blame Solley, too? She must have left that voicemail message before the fateful conversation with Dan.

"I hear you saying what Dan's doing is wrong," Janie said. "So have you spoken to Gin?"

"No, not yet." Solley had almost returned Gin's phone call numerous times over the past five days, but she was paralyzed. "I've been putting it off. What if she thinks I'm involved with the blackmail?"

"Gin's no fool. That scheme has Dan written all over it." Janie paused. She seemed to be measuring her words carefully. "Have you made a decision yet?"

Solley knew what Jane was referring to. "We're through.

I talked to Dan earlier. Told her she can fight me all the way in court for the kids."

Janie let out a sigh. "You're doing the right thing." Then she giggled.

Solley frowned at the odd reaction. "Thanks for the sympathy."

Janie looked aghast. "I'm not laughing about the breakup. I was just thinking about her with the kids. I wonder how she's coping."

"It's been five days. She's probably in the fetal position by now."

They both laughed.

Janie shook her head. "Full-time parenting. That's a long overdue learning curve for her."

"I thought it might wake her up. Let her find out firsthand what she's really asking for if she wants to share custody for half the time."

"It's about time you kicked butt back. I take it Gin was the catalyst?"

"She made me take a chance," Solley answered quietly. "She gave me confidence to change."

It was true. If she came away with just one thing from her summer fling, it was a new sense of possibility. Gin had showed her the way a connection between lovers should be. She'd shown her what she could have, what she deserved. In a few days, she had given Solley back what Dan had spent years stripping away. And though she was gone, she had left Solley with a renewed feeling of self-worth.

"It's obvious she was more than a life coach," Janie said dryly. "The entire country has seen the photos. What about sucking tit with Gin?"

"Yeah, I sucked tit with Gin. Tit and a whole lot more." Solley met her sister's gaze squarely. "I'm sorry I didn't tell you all the details but it was rocky, right from the start. We were just helping each other through a hard time, and I wasn't sure it would be a good move."

She didn't want to reveal herself anymore, she already felt so raw and violated over the photos and Gin's abrupt departure. Solley felt herself well up. Terrified that if she started to cry she'd never stop, she grabbed an armful of towels and stuffed them into the washing machine. She was such a stupid woman to fall for someone like Gin. And the damage she'd done to both of them. Letting Dan creep into what little time they'd had together was like welcoming a serpent into Eden.

Janie softened, like her hand-washed woolens, and dragged her into a hug. "I'm sorry, Sol. I had the wrong idea. I thought you were fooling around with that little bitch in the dunes, and then when I saw those photos of you and Gin I was worried you were going to smash her to bits. She's such a good friend to me and Marsha, I guess I love her, too. She's the sister I always wanted."

"Bitch." Solley pushed her away. Trying to salvage some slivers of self-respect, she insisted, "Gin and I weren't serious, you know. It just happened. I don't regret it and I hope she doesn't, either. But we've both moved on."

Except that Gin was returning and Solley would soon have to tell her these things herself, and sound convincing. But at what cost?

"You know what I don't understand? Why would Dan think Gin is emotionally invested enough to pay out that kind of money for you and the kids?" Janie frowned. "I don't mean to be cruel, Sol, but if it wasn't serious, there's no leverage, so I don't know why you're worried."

"Dan understands the business. The publicity problem is—"

"Bullshit," Janie completed firmly. "Gin's a noble person.

She left because she thought she was in the way of your custody battle. And if she allows herself to be blackmailed, I guarantee publicity is not a factor. She's never denied being lesbian, and who cares if there's gossip about a stuntwoman?"

Solley was silent, unwilling to explore the sticky subject of Gin's feelings, let alone her own.

Janie wasn't quite done with her. "I can see why you're nervous about Gin coming. You've got some major explaining to do. I hope you're not planning to let her be exploited."

"Of course not." With an indignant snort, Solley poured laundry detergent into the machine and turned on the wash cycle. "I'm going to tell her not to give Dan a dime."

"And?"

Solley avoided Janie's piercing gaze. Her sister saw far too much and Solley wasn't ready to expose her tender new feelings yet. She had to know, first, where she stood with Gin. A shiver of anticipation rolled through her body. The thought of seeing Gin again made her weak. Whatever happened, she knew she wouldn't let this weekend pass without telling Gin the truth.

She'd fallen for her, and it was so much more than a fleeting attraction.

❖

Later, long after everyone else had retired, Solley sat alone on the veranda steps with a glass of wine, gazing up at the black velvet sky. With or without stars, the night sky reminded her of Gin Ito's eyes, inky black with the intensity of her emotion or exploding with a million points of light when she and Solley touched. *I wonder what she saw in my eyes when she touched me? Probably just ugly, raw lust and bottomless need.*

Staring out toward a waning moon on an ebbing tide, she

had never felt so small and alone. Not even through all the emotionally inert years with Dan, when only the kids had kept her going. Now she felt she had lost not only a lover, but a true companion who cared deeply for her family. Looking back to their brief weeks together, she realized she took and took from Gin and gave no love, kindness, or gentleness back. *You're such a loser, Solley Rayner. You're such a selfish fool. You've thrown it all away. What a sad cliché of a person.*

She hadn't understood how much Gin meant until it was too late. Reminders of her loss were everywhere, the jetty, the trailer camp, the bed where... *Stop it!* Life went on. She'd made her mistakes, and very soon, she would have to face Gin and pay for them. Except her heart didn't seem to understand accountancy. It couldn't swap columns or balance out her emotions fairly and squarely. She was always left with a deficit she would never really stop paying. And tonight she found herself on the brink of emotional bankruptcy.

What if she saw Gin again and just burst like a dam, and all the fears and sadness and loneliness spilled out? She would be left in tatters for the rest of her life. Running a hand over the warm wooden deck, she remembered this was where they'd first kissed. And what a disaster that turned out to be. She laughed ruefully, feeling the sting of bittersweet tears burning behind her lids.

A car door slammed at the front of the house. She hadn't even heard it approach, she was so caught up in her maudlin thoughts. Quickly she wiped her damp lashes, scrabbling for decorum. Footsteps crunched toward the back deck. She knew they were Gin's before they even turned the corner. *When did I learn the weight of her tread, the pace of her step?*

She sat gazing fixedly out at the shore, feeling the other's hesitation. Neither of them spoke for what seemed like an eternity but must have been mere moments. Solley dared not break her gaze and turn around, not until she felt she had some sort of control. But what little she possessed was disintegrating like the waves on the shoreline.

"Solley?" The quiet voice that haunted her every hour came from behind. "It's me."

Still she sat in fragile silence, her heart drumming so hard she thought her ribs would splinter. She couldn't trust herself to speak for she knew her voice would break like glass.

"Is everything okay?" Gin asked.

"It is now." The words spilled out along with a shaky breath. "Everything is all right now."

Gin bent and took her hand. "Walk with me?" Her finger brushed Solley's lips as they parted to speak. "Shh. Let's just walk. I want to show you something very important. Come and share a secret with me."

CHAPTER FOURTEEN

It's beautiful up here," Solley breathed, looking along the shore and over to Janie's house. "What a view. I didn't even know this beach track existed, and I've been coming here forever." Behind her a wider lane led to the top of the rise and onto the main route out of Topaz Bay. It was a wonderful setting.

"This is where I'm going to build my home," Gin said quietly. "I've bought the land. Look over there. The foundations are being laid next month. It's going to be a two-story glass and timber frame, built to blend in with the environment. My sister, Miu, is an architect. She designed it and she's taken full control of the build for me." She couldn't keep her excitement out of her voice.

"That's wonderful. It's so right for you." Solley smiled warmly.

They stood side by side in silence, soaking up the moonlight shimmering over the bay below.

"Did Marsha mention about the stunt academy we're planning on opening?" Gin asked.

"No, when's this happening?"

"Wow, I can't believe she managed to keep it a secret.

Hopefully near the end of the year, if we get the paperwork together and clear up all our commitments."

"Tell me more."

"There's a sequel in the pipeline...*Revenge 3: Red's Return*. Janie and Marsha got another location deal for it. So, between us, we have the funds to get our academy dream up and running."

"That's great news."

"It's a relief. I'm getting too old for...plummeting."

Gin shot a sly sideways glance to see if Solley remembered using the word to describe Gin's profession. She was rewarded by a narrowing of glittering green eyes that set her heart pounding.

"Those tired old bones need to settle down, hmm? I think a stunt academy is an excellent idea. Especially with the skill set you and Marsha have between you."

Silence settled between them again, comfortable and familiar. Taking a deep breath, Solley reached for Gin's hand. She could feel her brow creasing with worries and regret. "Gin, I'm sorry."

"Don't," Gin murmured. "You don't have to explain anything."

"I want to." Solley pressed on, determined not to take the easy way out, even if Gin was willing to let her off the hook. "I never gave you any tenderness or consideration, or even had a thought for what you were going through. I just took everything I could to feed my own insecurities. And it wasn't until you'd gone and...and I thought I'd lost you, that I realized how important you'd become. I know it sounds clichéd not to appreciate someone until they've gone, but believe me, it's true. I was stupid. And greedy and scared, and utterly selfish."

Her faltering confession was halted as Gin's hand rose to cup her cheek. "I love you."

The three simple words silenced Solley, even as the whole world roared in her ears in one voice.

"I love you," Gin repeated. "I missed you so much, even though we'd barely begun. As soon as the plane took off, I knew I'd made the biggest mistake of my life. I should never have run. I should have stayed and tried to work it out with you." Her small smile became rueful. "I was a fool to think, for even one moment, that distance from you would free me. I'm bound to you, Solley. I need you in my life, if it is to have any quality, any meaning."

"Oh, Gin," Solley whispered in return. "I'm in love with you, too."

It was out there, in the real world, in full view, her love for this woman. And she knew it was a forever kind of love. This woman standing before her had more than proved her love and affection for her children, and was now expressing her love and commitment to Solley, and to a possible future together. She knew she could no more turn away from this than she could take back her own heartfelt words. Her loss had been absolute, but now, all had been returned to her tenfold. She had Gin back in her life and in her arms, and this time she would hold onto her tenderly and lovingly, safe in the knowledge she would never, ever let her slip away again.

"You love me?" Gin couldn't believe what she had heard, the whispered words she had secretly prayed for. She had come prepared to storm a citadel, only to find her love reflected back. "Oh, Solley, you've no idea how much I'm drowning in love for you. I was told once true love steals you forever. And I believe it."

Gin watched, aghast, as two big, fat tears rolled slowly

down Solley's cheeks. Carefully she kissed one then the other away, before stealing across to Solley's soft full lips.

Their kiss began softly as they shyly tasted one another. Gin sighed as Solley's tongue gently smoothed her lips, then timidly moved deeper. They both groaned, and Solley buried her hands in Gin's short hair. She felt Gin's arms encircle her waist as her lips traveled a familiar trail from earlobe to collarbone.

Nipping and sucking, inhaling the musk of Solley's skin, Gin gathered her into her arms and laid her carefully on the sand-dusted foundation of her new home. Stretching out beside her, she kissed across the soft fabric of her blouse and slowly unbuttoned it. Her tongue danced across the exposed skin to the sensuous swell cupped in delicate lace.

"I didn't tell you before, Solley, and I should have. Your body is so beautiful to me, so full of creamy curves and secret honeyed places. And your scent, it drives me wild. I adore the smell of your skin. And the taste of you."

Her lips trailed hot kisses down Solley's quivering belly. Unceremoniously, she pulled Solley's skirt up over her hips, bunching it at her waist. Instinctively Solley lifted her legs to wrap around the taut, strong body. Her breathing was ragged as her hips started to rock.

Here, on the hillside of La Sirena Verde, cradled in the sand and grass overlooking the starlit sea, barely focusing on the stars twinkling above, Solley's body hummed with delight. It felt so natural, so right to give her all to the woman who held her as if she was the most precious thing in her world.

"You are so, so beautiful," Gin murmured, peeling away Solley's panties, freeing her aroma into the night air. She growled and swooped to claim the scented sex.

Solley cried out at the intensity of the urgent tongue as it burrowed deep. She burned and throbbed, her petaled folds slick with honey. She fiercely ground her hips into Gin's mouth, riding her, seeking release. A thick tongue swept over her swollen clitoris, pulling it into a greedy mouth, where it was tugged on mercilessly.

Again and again, this sucking, plunging pleasure beat into her remorselessly, giving no quarter. The buildup to her release thundered from afar like a growing tsunami. Back arching, belly pushing up toward the sky, she convulsed as a huge orgasmic wave surged through her singing body, exploding in a thousand different directions. Tears streamed down her face, and deep, racking sobs shook her as emotional release followed the physical.

"I'm here, baby. I'm here. I love you, I love you. Don't cry." Gin crawled up and gathered her in her arms. Kissing her forehead with damp lover's lips, she brushed her cheeks clear of teardrops.

"I'm sorry. I'm sorry." Solley sniffled, curling into her lover's arms. "I don't know what's wrong...because...I'm actually very, very happy." Another rush of tears spilled down her face, followed by a hiccupping sob.

"Shh. That was a big one. It's bound to make you a little wobbly."

Gin helped her arrange her clothes and they snuggled back down in the dunes, unwilling to return to reality just yet. They lay cocooned in each other's arms, gazing up at the heavens, sure that tonight every star shone for them alone. "I think we've rescued each other, Solley. It feels so right to be here with you. I've waited so long for love to come back into my life. Sometimes I thought my only knowledge of it would be Miki's smile. But this summer everything was different... with you. And I nearly blew it, because I stupidly thought the right thing to do was to walk away and leave you and the kids with Dan."

"God, Dan and the kids…" Solley reluctantly focused on real life after the stupor of their lovemaking.

"It'll be okay. I've helped Dan out financially. I can do more. Just tell me what you need and I'll do it. I'll help any way I can."

Solley rolled onto her side to face Gin, head resting on her palm. Tension invaded her. She could feel her frown deepening. "You helped Dan out?"

"Yes, I brokered the deal she wanted. I have a little clout at the studio end. I thought you knew."

She was so matter-of-fact, Solley could almost believe the deal was friendly and casual. "No."

"Dan said she was staying in LA for the kids' sake, but she needed a guarantor and cash injection to secure her business and your financial security as a family. So I helped her out. In exchange, she dropped the lawsuit threats and the custody crap against you."

In a way, it had been a business deal like any other, except that the small print had scoured her heart until it bled. The irony wasn't lost on her; she was still bitter that the situation she'd instigated made it necessary for her to walk away from what she wanted most.

"She told me she got an unexpected guarantor and that she could do the deal. God, I was so happy when she shut up about that blackmailing nonsense." Solley's temper began to rise like mercury on a hot morning. In frustration, she said, "I wish you'd talked with me first. How could you give her all that money?"

"I saw you in the bedroom with her at Janie's that night. So I wasn't surprised when Dan told me you were both going to try again," Gin explained softly.

"What?" Solley bolted upright, more and more horrified. "Dan told you that?"

Gin sat up, too, unsure of the anger sparking off Solley. "She's a dung beetle, but she's also a shrewd businesswoman. I knew she could provide well for you all if she closed this deal. It was the best gift I could think of. A safe, prosperous future for you all."

"Gin, Dan and I decided to try and raise our kids together, but we're not a couple. We shared a deathbed that night. There's nothing left to be patched up, even if I wanted to try. And I don't."

"Does Dan know that?" Gin recalled Dan's self-satisfied pronouncements. According to her, Solley came crawling back on her hands and knees, desperate for them to be reunited.

Solley tried not to sound sarcastic. "Dan knows exactly how I feel about her."

"She said you two were talking about having an open relationship."

"That whore of a bitch. Where's my damned cell phone?"

"Huh?"

But Solley had leapt to her feet and was charging back down the track toward Janie's house, like a fiery streak of lightening, like a trailing comet, like Judgment Day.

CHAPTER FIFTEEN

Sniper felt less than happy. She was sat on a chair on the deck surrounded by Gin Ito, Solley, Janie, Grace, and Marsha Bren, and she didn't even have a camera in hand to mark this auspicious occasion. Normally she'd have lain in the sand until she took root to get a snap like this. Now all her gear was piled up on the deck behind psycho-bitch Grace Rayner, whose hot'n horny acquaintance she'd made two days ago.

Since then, her nether regions felt like they'd been scoured by sandpaper. Her flesh screamed for some soothing gel, but despite the raw discomfort, a very warm tingle rose deep in her belly every time she glanced at the younger Rayner. Shit, she had the hots for her, and that meant trouble. They'd only had a few rolls in the hay, or in this case, the dunes, over the last two days, and it was already obvious that Grace would be really, really bad for her.

Sniper didn't want to be here having Saturday brunch with the terrifying sisters, but she had her career to think about and Grace had promised to get her an exclusive. All she had to do was apologize and she would be invited to the cast and crew party tonight. She shifted uncomfortably at the thought of groveling. A trickle of sand escaped the leg of her shorts and pooled on the decking, leading to a knowing smirk from Grace and narrow-eyed annoyance from her older sister.

"Sniper just wants to apologize to everyone for the trouble she caused with her dirty-rat snooping," Grace began hastily. "Don't you, Sniper?"

"Huh? Oh, yeah. Sorry."

"Sorry what?"

"Sorry for all the dirty-rat snooping stuff," she mumbled, chin on chest. Fuck, half of them were kung fu experts. What if they thumped her to death and got the dog to bury her in the sand?

"And you especially want to apologize to Solley for the porno crap that she's had to endure, don't you?"

"It's okay." Solley held Sniper's eyes steadily. "No harm done. Forgive and forget is what I say." Grace frowned at this unusual graciousness. She wanted Solley to lose it. She wanted blood and snot. Where was Sol the Avenger?

Janie did not necessarily want blood and snot on her decking, but she, too, thought Solley had been uncharacteristically generous to the photographer. Catching the look that passed between Solley and Gin, she was even more bewildered. Ever since Gin had arrived two nights ago, they'd both been in some kind of dream state, oblivious to the events around them.

Marsha, big-hearted as ever, felt for the young woman so beleaguered by Rayner women. She knew firsthand what that felt like. "So, what are you going do to make it up?" she asked, moving the conversation in a more positive direction.

Sniper was confused. After Grace's demands, she had little left to give if this was going to get kinky. And having just spent weeks spying on these people, she knew she couldn't give them an inch.

"Dunno," she responded sullenly.

"I'll tell you what you can do," Marsha said. "You can

be the official photographer for this party. We decide on distribution and you get a thirty percent cut."

"Forty," Sniper bargained, trying to look her gift horse in the mouth even as it trampled her into the ground.

"Thirty-five, take it or leave it. I can always call around for another photographer."

"No, no. I'm in."

Sniper brightened. This sounded like a deal with good future options. No one else would have this scoop. It was an insider one-off, and she needed a break since Kelly Rose blew her off. All in all, from what she knew of this family, her fate could have been a hell of a lot worse.

Marsha offered a bone-crushing handshake. "Grace is your assistant tonight. One step out of line and we'll unleash her. You only photograph what you're told to. Got it?"

Janie rose. "Now go get washed up and changed. We're having a barbeque tonight and you're invited to eat with us. Grace, show Sniper to a room…somewhere." She gave her sister a long, hard look that said, *I know what you're up to*, before turning to Sniper one last time. "And get that sand out of your shorts. I don't need my floors looking like the damn Sahara."

"Come on." Grace put her hand on the small of Sniper's back. "I'll run you a bath, and I've a nice aloe vera salve parts of you might be interested in."

❖

Early in the afternoon, Dan's Beemer wound its way down to La Sirena Verde and pulled up in front of Janie and Marsha's home.

"Mommy!" Della's bellow announced her arrival before she'd even exited the car. "Jed called me a bitch."

"I did not. Della said 'crap.'"

"Liar."

"Get your kids away from me," thundered Dan as soon Solley appeared on the front veranda. "I have a blistering migraine. They haven't shut up since we left." She clasped a hand dramatically to her forehead.

Solley shook her head in exasperation as the kids charged past her into the house. "What are you doing here? It's only been five days, and they've broken you?"

"You don't understand. They keep ganging up on me."

"'Bitch' and 'crap'? That's the language they're learning while you're in charge? You know we don't curse in front of them. They're like parrots."

"I wasn't cursing, I was driving."

Solley glared at her. "This is not what we agreed. I'm supposed to be having at least a week alone to enjoy the party and catch up with Grace."

"With Gin Ito hanging around, I think you're catching up with a whole lot more."

"And your point?"

"Did you think you could just call me up and bite off my ear about taking her money?"

"The money wasn't the issue, although I'm not happy about that either. But you lied to her about us."

Solley couldn't bear to imagine what might have happened if Gin hadn't come back for the party. They could have spent months apart, with Gin keeping her distance out of a misguided respect for Solley's supposed relationship.

Dan's expression was unrepentant. "I had to tell her we were trying to make a go of it or she wouldn't have paid up."

"I can't talk to you," Solley said, appalled. "Just go home. Leave the kids here."

"Forget it. I'm not turning around now and driving all the way back. I'm exhausted."

"And you wanted them for six months of the year? Are you mad?"

"On the brink of it." Dan glanced around as Marsha directed the events company crew. They were rigging up lights. "Is Kelly Rose coming tonight?"

"Oh, I get it. You're here to gatecrash this party and network like a fishing trawler."

Will ambled up and gave her a big hug. "Missed you, Mom."

"Honey, is that nail varnish you've on?" asked Solley as she hugged him in return. Out of the three, he would always be her hugger.

"Yeah, I'm going to grow them," he answered happily before wandering into the kitchen after his brother and sister.

"It kept him quiet." Dan pointed to her head. "Look, I'm dying here. I need to lie down to ease this migraine."

"You can use my room." Solley said reluctantly. "But don't get too comfortable."

"Do you still have that eye mask, the one you can put in the freezer?" Whining and needier than the kids, Dan followed Solley into the cool of the house.

❖

The events company was adding the finishing touches to the marquee that now extended out from the decking in one continuous flow of party lights, bandstand, and dance area. Buffet tables stood dressed to the side, awaiting the arrival of the caterers.

"I'm so excited," Grace enthused. "I'm glad you didn't go for a theme." She stood with Sniper, examining the decor.

"I feel so sick I could throw up," Janie said nervously. Mass entertaining was not her thing.

"Now *that* would be a theme. A vomitorium party."

Sniper's wisecrack fizzled as she caught Janie's glare. Quickly she returned to fiddling with her camera.

Gin returned from her run to the other side of the bay, satisfied with the plans she was making for the coming year. It was a bonus that the stunt academy planning would keep her in this area for the rest of the month. Then, by the time she'd finished the Vancouver shoot, her house would be well underway. She sighed in contentment. She felt so at peace in this little cove. It was magical. She could think of no better place to start really living again.

Slipping into the house, she hurried upstairs for a quick shower before joining the others for a pre-party drink. At the top landing she hesitated, seeing Solley's bedroom door ajar. Imagining she could faintly smell her cologne and unable to stop herself, she moved quietly to the doorway, drawn by a tantalizing glimpse of a negligee draped over a chair, a discarded summer sandal.

There, sprawled on her belly across Solley's bed, her half naked body covered by only the thinnest sheet, lay Dan. What was that using bastard doing in Solley's bed? Gin's heart lurched in disbelief. With a sharp intake of breath, she slowly backed away from the sleeping woman. Her withdrawal was hampered by the sudden appearance of Nelson at her heels. With a wag of his floppy red tail, he ambled past her into the room and hopped onto the bed beside the sleeping woman.

Gin held her breath, waiting for Dan to wake and catch her hovering like a thief. Nelson proceeded to drop two well-placed, sloppy licks across Dan's mouth and cheek before curling up to snooze alongside her.

Gin couldn't prevent an evil grin, but her amusement was soon squashed when, without waking, Dan murmured into the furry head, "Sol?"

❖

"What's she doing in your bed?" Gin hissed like a fury. She had pounded downstairs to find Solley on the veranda with Grace and Sniper.

"Who? Dan?" Solley was stunned at her lover's vehemence. "She's sleeping off a migraine. Jesus, what did you think? Don't you trust me?" Her quick-fire temper flared.

Gin was momentarily appeased, but she pushed on belligerently. Seeing Dan in Solley's bed had pushed buttons she didn't even know she had. Jealousy burned off her like a satellite on reentry. "Well, what's she even doing here?"

"Babysitter whiplash." Solley and Gin were almost nose to nose in their stand off. "Why, did you think your check had bounced?"

"What the hell is that supposed to mean?"

"It means Dan may have blackmailed you, but it doesn't mean you own me. You didn't buy me. I don't care what she said about open relationships."

"What's going on?" A stressed Janie appeared beside Grace and Sniper, who shrugged in confusion.

"Dunno, sis. They just started clubbing each other."

"Stop it, you two. I don't need a domestic incident before guests start arriving." Janie's fretful tone brought Marsha out to see what was annoying her wife. Strident voices began to rise as each bickered over the other.

"This is not a domestic. We're not together," Solley informed Janie.

"We are together," Gin yelled.

"You fucking red-haired bastard," Dan roared. "I'm gonna kill you."

In the stunned silence all eyes turned to Dan, who was wiping her mouth on the T-shirt that hung over her briefs. Nelson pranced at her side, trying happily to trip her up.

"Fucking furball had his putrid tongue in my mouth,"

Dan complained. "I'm diseased. We all know what he does with it."

"Why the hell did you let him do that? And what did I tell you about language?" Solley scolded angrily.

"I thought it was your tongue. And I only cursed because this is an emergency."

"What? You thought it was me?"

"See!" Gin spat.

"Solley, what's going on here?" Janie asked, hands on hips.

"Well, I was half asleep and I saw the red hair," Dan spluttered defensively. "At least it explains the breath."

"If Gin thumps her, can I take pictures?" Sniper whispered to Grace. It was a once in a lifetime opportunity to snap the famous Gin Ito pounding on Marsha Bren's evil twin.

"But you still thought she was in bed with you—" Gin accused.

"Oh, fuck off, Grasshopper. Is that why you're looking daggers at me? You thought we were still together?"

"You told me you were."

"Hey, if you're so keen to be the new daddy, you can mind the kids for the rest of the week." Dan stabbed an indignant finger in Solley's direction. "And take her. The farther away from me the better. That madwoman spat seven levels of hell into my ear on the phone the other night because *you* brokered a deal with me. That was meant to be private."

"There are no secrets in this family," Solley declared self-righteously.

"No secrets, huh? Marsha, Janie, and I had a threesome." Dan pointed at a mortified Janie. "Bet she never told you about that."

"It was years ago," Marsha blurted.

Janie glared at her.

"What?" the others rhymed in a stupefied chorus.

Janie turned anxiously to Solley, scrabbling for damage control. "It was before you and Dan even met."

"You holier-than-thou tramp!" Solley howled, outraged.

"Hey, my sisters swing like lemurs," Grace snorted, amused that her siblings were sliding off the soapboxes they so often preached to her from.

"Oh, you hypocrite, after the covering-up I did for you last week." Janie railed against Solley's slur. "Sol humped Sniper in the sand dunes."

"What?" another chorus of disbelief rang out.

"I never did," Solley gasped.

"You humped my sister?" Grace bellowed at Sniper who blanched, then panicked.

"No. No. But I helped her set up the Rayner Terror Web site," Sniper confessed, because that, of course, made everything better.

"A Web site?" Gin looked aghast.

Dan looked proud.

"A Web site?" Janie echoed. She looked bilious.

"Well, there was money to be made with all the gossip and rumors. Why should I be the one constantly exploited?" Solley tried to sound justified.

"Yes, instead exploit everyone else," Janie snapped.

The gaggle of voices rose again.

"Enough!" Marsha commanded hands raised in the air. "I got the kids in the family room with ice cream and a stack of DVDs. The rest of you go get ready. This party is happening and people will be arriving soon. Go go go."

❖

The party was a resounding success. The movie was going to be a box office winner and spirits were high. Sniper was in her element, being able to freely move around and snap people she would normally never get within a million miles of, unless she crawled through their sewer pipe. She even had the authority to go up to some seriously famous faces and ask outright that they crush up close and pose for her. Paparazzi heaven.

Grace's interpretation of assistance was to sit back and watch her work, a satisfied smile on her lips. Sniper knew if she took one step out of line her ass would hit the sandbar in seconds flat. Truth was, she kinda liked the fact that she had at last met her match. It made her feel all warm and fuzzy inside.

Laughter and music floated across the surf as Gin and Solley stole away, after hours of dancing, to stroll up through the dunes and watch the sunrise. Snuggled together, they watched the light bloom over the horizon and the stars begin to fade. Gin gazed at the woman lying beside her. She took in the changing colors in the auburn hair as night crept away and dawn stole in. She marveled at the soft curve of Solley's cheek, the generous bowed lips, and the peachy fuzz of her earlobe. She had almost finished counting the bronzed eyelashes when Solley's eyelids fluttered and Gin found herself gazing into the lush green depths of her lover's eyes.

My lover's eyes are as green as a spring forest and they're looking adoringly at me, on what might be the first day of the rest of our lives.

"Good morning, Solley Rayner." She smiled shyly.

"Good morning, Gin Ito." Solley smiled back.

Gin leaned over and placed a soft kiss on Solley's mouth. "It's a new day and I love you more than ever."

Solley blushed in answer. "I love you," she whispered, realizing they now had many, many days to say these things to each other. "So, what shall we do with this new day?"

"Let's make plans." Gin snuggled against her. "About what Dan said last night—"

"The threesome? Yes, I was shocked, too—"

"No, dufus. About me child minding. About your family. I want to be part of that. I want a connection."

"Gin, you already have a connection. You're already in the kids' hearts."

"But I'm moving here, to La Sirena Verde. I'm building a house and opening a business. No more traveling. I'm making a home here, and I want it to be a family home."

"I'm glad you'll be near."

"Share it with me? Please? Let my house be a home for you and the kids. You can stay whenever you like, no pressure. I know you have to decide where you go from here, with your own life. But please, let me be a part of it. Let me help you and the kids."

Gin was worried she was pushing too far, too fast. But she wanted to be honest about her intentions from the start. "You know I love you. But it's more than that. I want you to be close, so we can grow into a new life together."

Her dark eyes locked with Solley's, pulling her into an unfathomable world of love and promise. Solley blinked, astounded by such a generous, loving act. "How can you offer me such unconditional love so soon? My life is a panicked mess. Day after day, my one goal is to keep things together. I love you so much, but you deserve better."

"No. I deserve you. We were two very unhappy people, Solley. Both lost in our hurt, struggling on with no real purpose, no destination. The universe has given us this chance to change things, and I'm going to grab it with both hands and squeeze every ounce of joy and love out of it. And you're going to do the same."

She caressed Solley's cheek with her thumb, marveling at the soft texture, smiling at the mischievous freckles, promising herself one day to kiss them all.

Solley gently leaned in to give the most generous mouth in the world the most tender of kisses. "Look," she murmured into the sweetness, "the sun's rising." She drew back slightly. "We can watch the sun rising on our new life together."

"Our new life together?" Gin raised an eyebrow.

"When I met you I promised myself I would be brave. I decided to reach out and try for happiness. And I did, and I fell flat on my face. But I got up and dusted myself down and tried again…and you came back." Solley nodded solemnly. "There's a big, scary world out there. But it seems less frightening with you in it, and positively friendly when you're by my side. But to have you as a lover and a partner, well, I could walk the length and breadth of it and always be smiling."

She stood and offered her hand to Gin. "Walk with me. Forever."

Standing with her, Gin said, "Forever? I like the sound of that."

With their hands warmly joined, they set out across the sand into the promise of a new day and a love that would guide them home.

About the Author

Gill McKnight works between Ireland and the UK. When she can grab some time she likes to hang out in the small house she is restoring in Greece. She likes sailing, gardening, and driving long distances with all her furniture in the back of a van.

Her next book, *Green-eyed Monster*, is due in December 2008 from Bold Strokes Books.

Books Available From Bold Strokes Books

Falling Star by Gill McKnight. Solley Rayner hopes a few weeks with her family will help heal her shattered dreams, but she hasn't counted on meeting a woman who stirs her heart. (978-1-60282-023-4)

Lethal Affairs by Kim Baldwin and Xenia Alexiou. Elite operative Domino is no stranger to peril, but her investigation of journalist Hayley Ward will test more than her skills. (978-1-60282-022-7)

A Place to Rest by Erin Dutton. Sawyer Drake doesn't know what she wants from life until she meets Jori Diamantina—only trouble is, Jori doesn't seem to share her desire. (978-1-60282-021-0)

Warrior's Valor by Gun Brooke. Dwyn Izsontro and Emeron D'Artansis must put aside personal animosity, and unwelcomed attraction, to defeat an enemy of the Protector of the Realm. (978-1-60282-020-3)

Finding Home by Georgia Beers. Take two polar-opposite women with an attraction for one another they're trying desperately to ignore, throw in a far-too-observant dog, and then sit back and enjoy the romance. (978-1-60282-019-7)

Word of Honor by Radclyffe. All Secret Service Agent Cameron Roberts and First Daughter Blair Powell want is a small intimate wedding, but the paparazzi and a domestic terrorist have other plans. (978-1-60282-018-0)

Hotel Liaison by JLee Meyer. Two women searching through a secret past discover that their brief hotel liaison is only the beginning. Will they risk their careers—and their hearts—to follow through on their desires? (978-1-60282-017-3)

Love on Location by Lisa Girolami. Hollywood film producer Kate Nyland and artist Dawn Brock discover that love doesn't always follow the script. (978-1-60282-016-6)

Edge of Darkness by Jove Belle. Investigator Diana Collins charges at life with an irreverent comment and a right hook, but even those may not protect her heart from a charming villain. (978-1-60282-015-9)

Thirteen Hours by Meghan O'Brien. Workaholic Dana Watts's life takes a sudden turn when an unexpected interruption arrives in the form of the most beautiful breasts she has ever seen—stripper Laurel Stanley's. (978-1-60282-014-2)

In Deep Waters 2 by Radclyffe and Karin Kallmaker. All bets are off when two award winning-authors deal the cards of love and passion… and every hand is a winner. (978-1-60282-013-5)

Pink by Jennifer Harris. An irrepressible heroine frolics, frets, and navigates through the "what ifs" of her life: all the unexpected turns of fortune, fame, and karma. (978-1-60282-043-2)

Deal with the Devil by Ali Vali. New Orleans crime boss Cain Casey brings her fury down on the men who threatened her family, and blood and bullets fly. (978-1-60282-012-8)

Naked Heart by Jennifer Fulton. When a sexy ex-CIA agent sets out to seduce and entrap a powerful CEO, there's more to this plan than meets the eye…or the flogger. (978-1-60282-011-1)

Heart of the Matter by KI Thompson. TV newscaster Kate Foster is Professor Ellen Webster's dream girl, but Kate doesn't know Ellen exists…until an accident changes everything. (978-1-60282-010-4)

Heartland by Julie Cannon. When political strategist Rachel Stanton and dude ranch owner Shivley McCoy collide on an empty country road, fate intervenes. (978-1-60282-009-8)

Shadow of the Knife by Jane Fletcher. Militia Rookie Ellen Mittal has no idea just how complex and dangerous her life is about to become. A Celaeno series adventure romance. (978-1-60282-008-1)

To Protect and Serve by VK Powell. Lieutenant Alex Troy is caught in the paradox of her life—to hold steadfast to her professional oath or to protect the woman she loves. (978-1-60282-007-4)

Deeper by Ronica Black. Former homicide detective Erin McKenzie and her fiancée Elizabeth Adams couldn't be happier—until the not-so-distant past comes knocking at the door. (978-1-60282-006-7)

The Lonely Hearts Club by Radclyffe. Take three friends, add two ex-lovers and several new ones, and the result is a recipe for explosive rivalries and incendiary romance. (978-1-60282-005-0)

Venus Besieged by Andrews & Austin. Teague Richfield heads for Sedona and the sensual arms of psychic astrologer Callie Rivers for a much-needed romantic reunion. (978-1-60282-004-3)

Branded Ann by Merry Shannon. Pirate Branded Ann raids a merchant vessel to obtain a treasure map and gets more than she bargained for with the widow Violet. (978-1-60282-003-6)

American Goth by JD Glass. Trapped by an unsuspected inheritance and guided only by the guardian who holds the secret to her future, Samantha Cray fights to fulfill her destiny. (978-1-60282-002-9)

Learning Curve by Rachel Spangler. Ashton Clarke is perfectly content with her life until she meets the intriguing Professor Carrie Fletcher, who isn't looking for a relationship with anyone. (978-1-60282-001-2)

Place of Exile by Rose Beecham. Sheriff's detective Jude Devine struggles with ghosts of her past and an ex-lover who still haunts her dreams. (978-1-933110-98-1)

Fully Involved by Erin Dutton. A love that has smoldered for years ignites when two women and one little boy come together in the aftermath of tragedy. (978-1-933110-99-8)

Heart 2 Heart by Julie Cannon. Suffering from a devastating personal loss, Kyle Bain meets Lane Connor, and the chance for happiness suddenly seems possible. (978-1-60282-000-5)

Queens of Tristaine by Cate Culpepper. When a deadly plague stalks the Amazons of Tristaine, two warrior lovers must return to the place of their nightmares to find a cure. (978-1-933110-97-4)